Parabolas

Focusing the Light

GUY MCCLUNG

WESTBOW
PRESS®
A DIVISION OF THOMAS NELSON
& ZONDERVAN

WestBow Press books may be ordered through booksellers or by contacting:

WestBow Press
A Division of Thomas Nelson & Zondervan
1663 Liberty Drive
Bloomington, IN 47403
www.westbowpress.com
1 (866) 928-1240

Scripture taken from the Douay-Rheims 1899 American Edition of the Bible.

ISBN: 978-1-9736-8356-8 (sc)
ISBN: 978-1-9736-8358-2 (hc)
ISBN: 978-1-9736-8357-5 (e)

Library of Congress Control Number: 2020900612

Print information available on the last page.

WestBow Press rev. date: 1/20/2020

Contents

Orphan.. 1

Ego Te Absolvo.. 4

Heal.. 13

End Human 25

Mercy 42

Postpersons.. 60

Indeed Fine Wine 62

Ranger.. 78

Orphan

░▒░

Through the fence, carefully, without touching it, she watched as so many friends—each holding a bag in one hand and certificate in the other—walked through the gate and boarded the bus. It was not one of those open-windowed, broken-down, yellow, oven-like hulks that had brought them to the Happy Land site, but one that was new and cool with closed windows misted over on the inside. She could see their forearms, each with the black cross and dull-blue number changed to a row of colorful flowers. Each smiling face mirrored the happy face on his or her certificate as each child, now called by a new name, was handed a small box of candy while getting on the bus. She remembered what candy tasted like and felt her tongue moving in her mouth.

Their certificates proved they had memorized the required lines from The Book and had said them out loud before the entire assembly, to the satisfaction of the loving caregivers and their peers. Exuberant applause had followed each success, and muted groans had followed the failed ones who would have their chance—some their last chance—at the next assembly.

She had already failed at two Assembly meetings, not because she did not know the words, but because she refused to say them. She knew they were not true. The first time she'd stood on the dais, it had been her eleventh birthday. No one knew that. No one cared. Birthdays had been abolished.

Nobody asked where her copy of The Book was. No one noticed she no longer carried it all the time as did so many of the children. They had no idea that she had dealt with the rationing of Happy Land toilet paper and her case of dysentery by making good use of the pages. She smiled when she thought of using the page with the title "Dreams of Myself" and the image of the Leader—his malevolent, dark face foreboding with assurance—as she folded the page in half.

"Honey, get it right this time. You know this is your last chance. We all want you to leave here happy," said a friendly serendipity assistant, ready to usher her onto the dais.

"Number 31231213," said the voice.

She stood up, walked onto the dais, and looked around the assembly hall. All the Happiness Brigade officers were lined up in the front row before her—women and men indistinguishable from each other in their brown uniforms and short haircuts. She saw her friend, Number 15315355, watching, hoping she could do it.

She thought of her mom and dad, what they had taught her, how they had hugged her, and their final I-love-yous that night as they were taken away. She wondered if she would be taken to them or if they were even still alive. Then she held her forearm up high, with the cross and her number facing forward, and with fist unclenched, she began. "I am not Number 31231213. I am Elizabeth Sarah McClure."

There were some muted intakes of breath along the front row.

She continued. "I am an American. I believe in God, the Father Almighty, Creator of heaven and earth, and in Jesus Christ, His only Son, our Lord ..."

The gasps from the audience made it hard to hear her. Front row officers, at first stunned, stood and cast accusatory glances at each other as they looked at the cameras; they knew this was being broadcast and recorded.

Some were vehemently gesturing toward the sides of the assembly hall. Security operatives materialized from everywhere.

As Elizabeth got to the words "suffered under Pontius Pilate, was crucified, died, and was buried. On the third day, He rose again from the dead," one angry operative threw her to the floor. As she said,

"I believe in the Holy Spirit," another operative covered her mouth, silencing her, while three others picked her up and hurried off the dais, holding her aloft as if they carried a corpse.

Number 15315355 stared in amazement. She had seen the operatives outside the fence, but never at an assembly.

After a few moments, she was gone. Quiet ensued. Everyone was seated. The voice said, "Number 56897977," and the next child stepped up on the dais. The child began, "I am Number 56897977."

- § -

Back in her tent, Number 15315355 wondered if she would ever see her friend again. She thought of her own name, Therese Jennifer Elder, and how her parents called her their "Little Flower." They had told her that the real-life "Little Flower" had been a saint. Assured no one was coming in, she removed the dirt and gravel from the wooden panel over the hole in the ground and took out the large book Elizabeth had given her. She opened it randomly and read, "In the beginning was the Word, and the Word was with God, and the Word was God ..." (John 1:1 KJV).

Ego Te Absolvo

The German shepherd puppy sat up by the gravestone. He heard the noises in the forest behind the old man. Then the old man heard branches moving and twigs breaking in the trees. He did not turn around.

The gravestone before him read simply, "Beloved Eva Anna 1912–1954." Encased in glass, an oil painting of a brilliantly lit Virgin Mary caressing the baby Jesus leaned against the stone, reflecting sunlight onto the old man's face. Only a bench and this grave occupied the hilltop. He stood in silence with his head bowed, resigned, waiting.

The dog stirred, looking at the trees and then back to the old man. A sparrow flew down and perched on the picture frame.

"Fuchsl, quiet. Stay. Still."

The dog obeyed and lay back down at the man's feet.

When the person was standing behind him, the old man turned and said in French, "It is time now, isn't it?"

The other man removed his overcoat. He was clad in a black cassock with a Roman collar, and he carried a Luger pistol in his hand. Monsignor Janek Odveta held his hand steady. He was tall. His hair was blond and his eyes, clear sky blue. He towered over the man sitting on the bench. He pointed the pistol at the old man's face. "You don't know who I am," he said in German, "but I have known you since that day in Lidice."

The old man responded in German. "Lidice. Yes, we thought the assassins of the man said to have an iron heart sought refuge there after his killing. We were wrong."

"Wrong? We? We were wrong! Lidice was innocent. The killers of the Butcher of Prague were not there. He had an iron heart and an iron soul. In all your propaganda after that, I never saw any newsreels of you with the men and boys lined up and an officer handing his Luger to you. Never saw a publicity photo of you there, killing the first two as they looked up at you. They were my father and my brother. And then it was as if you were never there."

The old man looked down. Then he looked up again. "I did that. No words of mine now can bring them back. Neither is there anything that could satisfy you or stop you now. Nor should there be."

"Satisfy? You either killed the women and children right there or sent them off to the camps—with four exceptions. My sister went alone because they saw my mother was pregnant. She and three others were the exceptions because they were with child. They were taken to the hospital, and in a storage room, without anesthetic, on the floor, abortions were performed on them. And they made sure these details were made public to everyone."

"I now know that and more," said the old man.

"This is that pistol." The priest pushed the Luger toward the old man, still holding it in front of his face. A small silver medallion with the SS runes and death's head embossed on each side dangled from a thin leather lanyard attached to the pistol.

The old man did not move.

"It was vacation. I was there, a seminarian home for a visit. When my parents heard the convoy arrive, they hid me in an attic overlooking the street. Then your huge black Mercedes drove up, and you exited like a conquering hero. They lined up all the men and boys. I saw it all. I saw the revenge in your eyes. This is the pistol that you used when you killed my father and brother. I was there!"

The old man remembered the report some days later about the officer who had handed him the pistol; his throat had been slashed, and the Luger was never found. The case was never solved.

"After that day in Lidice," said Janek, "I killed your officer with his own SS dagger. It had the word 'loyalty' etched into the blade. His oath to you is now meaningless, and none of those who swore to lay down their lives for you are here to protect you now."

The old man waited for the gunshot. It did not come. There was silence for a few moments. The sparrow flew up, landed on Eva's gravestone, and then flew away. "How did you find me? No one else has done so all these years."

"I learned to think like a German, a Nazi—plans, paranoia, pride. All three mean you kept minutely detailed records, files, ledgers, journals, diaries. Data and facts and reports are there for the finding. And I found them. But then I did what no else did. I put it all together."

"But how did you gather it all?" the old man asked.

"It was actually very simple," said the priest.

"As a then newly ordained Father Odveta, it was easy—very easy—for me, after the war, to have myself assigned to the new Vatican bureau for assisting in the rebuilding of churches and diocesan infrastructures all over Europe. Pope Pius XII was particularly interested in helping the Church to rise from the ashes of war, and the pope had heard of me. We became personal friends. I went all around Europe. My periodic reports were forwarded to the Holy Father, and sometimes he called me in to personally report to him. I had a gift with languages, which made it even easier for me to go where I wished. I was in a unique position to find you.

The old man looked up. "Yes, that Pope, that saint. He personally saved more people than anyone, all by himself, more than some countries did."

"I was looking for you," the priest continued. "The governments were not. The Church certainly was not. The allies and the Russians were frantic, cared much more about rocket scientists and jet engineers and the likes of the proteges of Hahn, Strassman, and Meitner. So ironic, wasn't it, that Lise Meitner was a Jew and her work made Little Boy and Fat Man possible? Those A-bombs ended the war for the Allies. Imagine how different things would have been had she been working for you."

There was sadness in the old man's eyes. He did not smile. "And we spent millions to insure Lise did not get the Nobel Prize she deserved with the others. Our perfidy and cunning were all encompassing," said the old man.

The old man saw the priest lower the pistol. He had reacted to the word perfidy.

The priest looked the old man in the eye. "And it was my understanding of that cunning and of that perfidy, and that it was, as you say, all encompassing, that helped me unravel the Doppelt Doppelt operation. Both the Allies and the Russians gave me carte blanche, and Pius the Twelfth."

"We thought no one knew. So you figured this out?"

"I had access to anyone and everyone, any and everywhere. They even had no problem with me going into prisons, even into the Soviet army's locations. The Russians even let me hear confessions— the Russians! In confession, a man tells everything. Nothing is held back, especially if he is to be executed, and I learned more than any interrogator, more than any torturer. I gathered and sifted and listed and compiled—like a good Nazi—more information than all of them put together about you, about Double Double. I knew you had not died in Berlin. That is not how you planned, how your ministers planned. More importantly, I came to see the plan of the first Doppelt operation, which some of them discovered, but then Doppelt Doppelt. I don't think anyone else noted the name change or gave it any significance if they did."

"Double Double," said the old man. "Yes, not two, but two and two, four of me. And four of Eva. Still, how did you do it?"

"I knew the lengths to which your men would go in their planning of anything. The trains to the camps were always on time. Each bullet was accounted for. Each gold filling from Auschwitz was weighed and listed. The pounds of hair cut from the prisoners before they were gassed were separated by colors—one color hair for the parts of the bomb fuses, one color hair for the submariners' socks. And to protect you, no detail ignored. There was no limit, no plan too farfetched, no expense too great, no one else who had to be saved at all costs, no one else who was not expendable. And I knew you would not die in Berlin or anywhere. Four feints, four rabbit trails, doubles for the Allies, doubles for Uncle Joe, doubles for Argentina, and doubles to roam, once seen to vanish. And you were none of them. You were gone."

The old man thought of the Reisender plan to save him and of his flight out of Germany in 1944 after the last counteroffensive in the Ardennes failed. "But what did you find? What convinced you?"

"The meticulous records of the Berghof. A tutor was hired at several hundred marks per month to teach the chef's children French. But they were already fluent in French when he arrived from Burgundy. So why French?"

The old man smiled. "You cannot plan everything. You cannot lie upon lie upon lie. So, it was the French lessons."

"Yes, and then where could you speak French and not stand out? Not France. Not any small country or colony around the world. Certainly no island. At first I went to French Guiana; but, after some time, and some interviews, then I realized—Quebec."

"And here we were, Eva and I, the whole time since we left America in 1946."

"I knew you were there—America. In the beginning you were in San Antonio, Texas. Did you know that, in its history, there were times when that city was almost half German?"

The old man nodded in agreement. Of course they knew, with their attention to details. That was part of the planning. He shook his head up and down as if to agree that the priest had gotten it right. "Yes, the Menger Hotel, the Alamo, and real beer. Still, now, here, how do you know it is me?"

The priest took a photograph from his pocket. It was of a child, an infant, clad in white and staring ahead. "The eyes." He showed the photograph to the old man.

"Yes, my mother, Klara, had that one taken."

"The eyes. And yours, even now, are the eyes of this child." The priest gestured at the painting with the Luger. "Mother Mary is holding you. Even though I have only seen copies, these are your eyes." The priest held the photo next to the painting's depiction of the Christ Child.

"The field marshal was so pleased when he presented it to me. He said, 'I return the masterpiece to the artiste.' You can see it is not great art. Yes, they are my eyes."

"Are you tired?" the priest asked the old man.

The old man looked surprised and then he replied, "May I sit?"

The priest pointed to the bench with the Luger. The old man sat down. The priest had watched hours, days, weeks of movies and video of this man; but the vehemence, the energy, the demonic fire was gone. The priest did not want to even hint at it, but this man was different.

"Good, good that we are here. I am here now because she saved me." The old man looked over at the stone with Eva's name. He went on. "All of them, they had the doctor and they thought they would have him prop me up, inject me, control me, show me off, and rule as my handlers, my puppeteers, as they thought they had done since 1938. She stood up to them. It was she who insisted that Dr. Warburg treat me."

"Warburg?" asked the priest. "Dr. Otto Warburg?"

"Have you heard of him? Did he turn up in your investigations?"

"Yes, Otto Heinrich Warburg, World War One hero, Nobel Prize in medicine, nominated forty-seven times, did cancer research. Received the Iron Cross for bravery. One of the greatest scientists Germany has ever produced. He treated you? I could never prove it."

"Yes, and that is why he survived. They knew he had cured me of cancer, a fact never publicized, and they knew that, because of that, he was untouchable."

The priest shook his head and smiled. "That explains so much that was, until this day, simply a puzzle to me."

"And he did indeed cure cancers. But the pharmaceutical companies feared what would happen to them if his research and results were given any credence. Someday he will be proven correct."

"And Eva found out about him and introduced you?"

"Yes. Then she was with me when we escaped. And she was with me when I went through Hades. Hades in Texas. For years I had taken the drugs daily, often ten times or more, over twenty different ones.

I wanted it, I demanded it, and they thought they could give them to me and move me around like a pawn on their chess board. No, I knew what I was doing. I did not say no. Then, as I screamed in the night, Eva held me, like in the painting. And then it was over. The drugs no longer had their hold on me. It took about two years. It was as if I had been reborn."

The priest was thoughtful. "And the handler's let you live?"

"Not one of them would be known as the killer of the dear, beloved leader. And they had their own problems. So we lived here at the bottom of the hill. She sewed." The old man touched the sewn edge of the scarf around his neck. "You know her mother was a seamstress and taught her daughter well. I painted and I walked and I read the papers."

The old man noticed the priest's silence. "So, you learned that, among the millions of facts you learned Franziska, Eva's mother, was a seamstress." The old man knew that continuing to talk would not mean that the priest would let him live.

"Your friend, the Pope. I read about your Pope since then. They have successfully smeared him. He was a courageous scourge to our plans. Politics exist even in the Vatican, sometimes especially in the Vatican; but he is a saint now whether they canonize him or not. He personally was responsible for saving thousands—no tens of thousands. And not only Jews, but priests, ministers, writers, intellectuals, and many others. And he had not one plane, no tanks, no U-boats, no guns. Many times I cursed him. Now I will look up to heaven and see him."

The old man paused, then he said, "Father, please hear my confession." The old man could see the disbelief in the priest's eyes. "I will understand if you refuse."

The priest sat down at the other end of the bench. He thought he could let this man die. He could kill him now, and he would go to his judgment unforgiven and then to a deserved eternal hell. God's mercy never trumped His justice. By refusing to hear him, the priest could see that he was damned forever. This would be so unlike the man's first confession those decades ago as a little boy with the shining eyes. And what could be the punishment for refusing him? Surely nothing serious. Surely this lost sheep was lost forever and of little account. He looked at the sparrow now flitting around the grave, and he remembered the recoil of the pistol, held in this man's hand, as his little brother's head exploded. He thought of the other millions, some whom only he had discovered. He would not let this prodigal son return. He had no birthright to claim. No savior to invoke. No God to call Father. No entry into the kingdom. Some sins were beyond forgiveness. The sparrow flew away.

The priest leveled the pistol inches from the old man's forehead. The old man did not move. He did not lower his head. For some moments the priest held the pistol there, and then he lowered it. He could not do it. Whether it was the grace of his ordination, the value denied to so many by this man, or the value he had seen in everyone he encountered after the war, the value of even this lost soul, he put the pistol down on the bench.

The priest made the sign of the cross and then began the words of the sacrament in German: "May the Lord be in your heart and help you to confess your sins with true sorrow."

The old man exhaled. "Bless me, father, for I have sinned. It has been many years since my last confession. These are my sins ..."

For well over an hour, the old man made a confession the likes of which the priest had never heard or imagined. He began to feel like Jesus carrying His cross to Calvary, the weight so overpowering he had to struggle to get up. He thought, Now I can refuse him absolution. Now he has admitted that he did these things. Now his hell will be insured.

The old man ended, "For these and all the sins of my past life, I am truly sorry."

The priest focused on the irony of that word, truly. What if he was lying? Truly? Is this possible for him? The image of Jesus with the woman to be stoned flashed before him, and he knew that he too was not without sin. Then he heard the words of the Good Thief, on his own cross. He heard the thief's confession as he was crucified and dying with Jesus. And he remembered Jesus's words after the thief proclaimed him Lord: "This day shalt thou be with me in paradise" (Luke 23:43 DR).

The priest stood and picked the Luger up with both hands. He looked at the pistol, with its death's head, and then he looked down at the old man. He reached into his pocket and took a handful of bullets and threw them past the gravestone. He looked at the pistol. He had known its chamber and magazine were empty. He threw it away from him, the death's heads flashing in the sunlight before it fell among the trees.

"Every day, for your penance, for the rest of your life, say the rosary and remember this: each time you say the words 'for us sinners,' you must include all the holy souls in purgatory."

Then he reached into his pocket and took out the rosary given to him by Pope Pius the Twelfth personally. He handed it to the old man. Then he intoned the words of absolution: "Dominus noster Jesus Christus te absolvat; et ego auctoritate ipsius te absolvo ab omni vinculo excommunicationis et interdicti in quantum possum et tu indiges." Making the sign of the cross, he continued: "Deinde, ego te absolvo a peccatis tuis in nomine Patris, et Filii, et Spiritus Sancti. Amen."

As he finished, the old man too made the sign of the cross. Two sparrows landed on the gravestone. Without a word, the priest turned and walked away.

By Adolf Hitler, 1913; Mother Mary With Child Jesus

Heal

The applause from lesser lawyers began as Garnth McClure Johnson finished his speech at the bar association luncheon. Although he had spoken on settling rather than prolonging litigation, his first thought was that he and the audience well knew what was unsaid—that settling meant you killed the cash cow. The lawsuit was over; the stream of regular invoices ran dry; and in-firm credit for providing work for a junior partner, two associates, two paralegals, and two assistants ended.

He never forgot filing a motion for summary judgment when he was a young associate at the instruction of a client's general counsel when the lead attorney on the case was unreachable, gone to some wilderness on vacation. On his return, it was as if a volcano erupted, "Do you realize that this is a good motion and it means this case is over?" yelled the partner.

Garnth's next thought was to have his resume updated with another entry in the public speaking section once he got back to his corner office.

- § -

His résumé. It was the detailed story of the legal life of Garnth McClure Johnson, basically his whole life for less than two years of law school and his eight years of legal practice. He had done all of law school—every course—at prestigious 'The' University of Texas, with honors, and he'd done it in a year and eleven months. He had never met anyone else who had ever accomplished that, especially while working at a part-time job and attending only those few classes in which the professor took roll. He had "Am Jured," receiving the highest grade in one of those classes that he had never attended.

But the résumé did not list what wrongs he had done and what good he had failed to do, or that he had greatly sinned, but only what he had done to further himself and, correlatively, make money. His clients could well attest to the money part.

He knew what he had billed out, what had been collected, and he knew what the senior partners decided was his share, their decision that defined "fair" having no appeal. And lately he had come to realize exactly how much of the fruits of his labors the senior partners were, in their view of "fairness," keeping for themselves. He saw that they did not work; rather, they "administrated." They did not take into account or share with him the collections from the litigation matters he generated but on which he did not personally work. He knew that, although some of them rarely worked an actual billable hour, each month they put a quarter of an hour down as "review file" on every file they supervised, which meant they had impressive levels of billable time.

So, the résumé. He needed to make it current for the new job search he was about to begin so he could find a much fairer sharing of what he accomplished. The document would highlight his more than four years of being "first chair" as an associate—something remarkable for one so young—and making partner in six years— something unheard of in the new legal industry in which most young attorneys never made partner. It was an industry that had seen the demise of the "pyramid" model of getting rich from the law.

That old business model had been replaced by a pull-the-ladder-up-behind-you mentality, which meant you tried to see to it that almost no one ever made partner after you did. It was not uncommon for a section head to award himself or herself all the end-of-year promotion points that should have been spread around the partners in a section. Many recently made partners who, in effect, received no promotion, left the firm the following January after their Christmas bonus checks had cleared the bank.

He was pleased. His résumé reflected his superiority, his many gifts: intelligent, aggressive, focused, poised, creative, professional, insightful, persuasive, discreet, effective—a winner. He laughed. Should he spell it profe$$ional? Yes, he was gifted, and now it was time for those gifts, his gifts, to be appropriately acknowledged.

Many worked and invoiced 25/8 rather than 24/7. Using the concept of "value billing," the same work could be billed to more than one client, which made the day more than twenty-four hours long. Under this sort of schedule, there was little time for that Third Commandment: Keep holy the Lord's Day. The firm—that is, the senior partners—defined "holy" as "profitable," and the only Lord was bottom-line in dollars. The Lord's Day was a servile labor day, an extra day of billable hours, and "rejoice always" meant, as the commandant of the prison camp at the Bridge on the River Kwai had said, "Be happy in your work." Garnth had often smiled when he heard of his peers boasting about billing three thousand hours a year. That was nothing compared to his thirty-six hundred or more. Some years he had worked each of its three hundred and sixty-five days.

He recalled Geoffrey Lamont McLarmond, who had billed out more hours one year than he had, and amazingly had won a first-chair patent infringement case as a four-year associate, a case every partner thought would be a loser. But Geoffrey made a mistake, a number of mistakes. On several occasions, senior partners saw him joking around with some non-attorney personnel, and once he'd been guilty of helping the office supply people move some boxes of paper on a dolly. After billing more than thirty-four hundred hours that year, his year-end review was simply that he was getting a bonus and that he was seen as being too friendly with non-attorney personnel. He was gone in two months.

- § -

In his office, in a corner of the forty-ninth floor of The Law Tower, Garnth sat down and clicked the email icon on his computer screen.

But then, when he went to move the cursor, a pain shot through his hands, as he cried out, "Arrgghhhgh!"

He got up, realized his feet and his side were also in pain, and staggered out the door to his assistant's station. "Look at these," he almost shouted, holding his hands up for her to see, bending over a partition and extending his hands over her computer, blood flowing onto the screen.

Judith Germone was one of the best executive assistants in the firm. Garnth called them secretaries, and because of his status, no one corrected him. She was the sixth assistant who had worked for him. She had lasted almost a year, which was a record.

A very senior partner had once remarked about his reputation as the "drivingest" of slave drivers, the most inhumane to the subhuman non-attorneys in the firm. Garnth had taken that as a compliment.

"Yes?" she asked.

Garnth realized she saw nothing unusual. He stared at her staring at his hands. She reached out and held one of his hands that was outstretched to her.

In that moment, Garnth knew her; her thoughts and feelings flowed into him. He knew what she was going through at home, her suffering with an alcoholic husband, her own health problems, her young son's recent fight at school, and her concern for her mother who had recently been placed in an assisted living facility. She was worried about getting there to see her that night. His pain increased as he became aware of her burdens. He saw her look up at his face, knowing she must his pain. Then he felt a soothing glow flowing to her. It was peace.

He watched her as she looked up, her face a question. Then he realized she could not see what was happening. He composed himself, and the pain began to ease.

"I thought maybe they might look weird to you," he said, not knowing what else to say so she would not think he was losing it or hallucinating. He turned and went back into his office, hoping she did not say anything to anyone about this.

He saw her sit upright in her chair and blink her eyes. Then he saw her smile.

Back at his desk, the pain stopped. The wounds in his hands, feet, and side healed in moments, and the blood disappeared. He was stunned.

- § -

Pain awakened him the next morning, a Sunday. Pain in his hands, pain in his feet. He did not know how he got dressed, got in the car, and drove to a twenty-four-hour emergency care center.

A young child was there who evidently had broken an arm. The forearm was nearly bent double, and the child was losing consciousness as a result of the pain. As Garnth walked toward the receptionist, the child, although supported by his father, toppled toward Garnth. Catching the child, touching him as the child cried out in pain, Garnth again felt his pain increase as it had when Judith held his hand. He began to see the accident in which the child had been injured. He'd fallen from a tree while trying to retrieve a bird's nest. Clutching the nest instead of trying to stop his fall, he'd fallen with the nest and his arm doubled up under him. Garnth teared up when he saw the child crying in his father's arms. An X-ray technician asked father and son to go with her down the hallway.

Eyes wide open, the child stood up beside Garnth, staring at him and then at his arm. The arm was now straight. The child was no longer in pain.

His father took the arm in his hands and turned it over and back. "Could it have just been dislocated?" he asked the X-ray technician.

"Sir, that is really curious," said the technician. He too had seen the arm when the child was brought in, and he could see it now. "I'm no doctor, but I know that arm was broken."

Garnth leaned against the wall in agony; but as the child and his father walked down the hallway, Garnth's pain subsided. Still, he had to find out what was going on. He approached the receptionist. "I'll pay by check rather than using my insurance," he told her. No one was to know about this.

She walked with him down a short hallway to a treatment room.

I guess she cannot see all the dripping blood, he thought.

The young doctor on call came in and asked him what was wrong.

Again, Garnth could tell that the doctor saw nothing. "My hands and feet are killing me—shooting pains as if someone is driving huge nails through them," he said, holding up his hands and motioning toward his feet.

The doctor inspected his hands, touching each finger, then the palms. Then he turned them over. Garnth's pain got worse, and he sensed that the doctor was troubled by thoughts of a broken marriage. He saw three beautiful children, all young, running around a trampoline in a backyard, laughing as they tried to catch their dad, this doctor. He saw their mom at a window, smiling as she watched her family. As the doctor continued to hold his hands and then his feet, Garnth's pain lessened.

When the doctor took Garnth's hands in his, again Garnth knew his life was going to be fine.

The doctor stared at Garnth's hands. "Just now, something very unusual happened. I felt heat and light and energy, and then … This is hard to put into words … a peaceful feeling." The doctor continued to stare at Garnth's hands. "Do you use a keyboard a lot?"

"Not so much as I used to," Garnth said.

"Do you work out a lot? Running? Cycling?"

"Well, yes, whenever I can, but that has been less frequently lately."

The doctor examined Garnth's feet and then his hands again.

"I think," said the doctor, "even though you are relatively young, this could be early onset osteoarthritis. Am I right that, as I manipulated your hands, the pain decreased?"

"Well, not at first. It actually got worse. But then, yes, it did feel better." Garnth thought this doctor simply had no clue about what was going on. And the doctor had not mentioned the blood. Garnth could not believe he could not see the blood.

"Let's try this," said the doctor. "I am going to prescribe some mild arthritis pain medication. Follow the directions on the bottle, and if this flares up again, come on back in, even if it is in a few days. If we have to, then we will take some X-rays and see if there is anything more serious."

- § -

Garnth parked his BMW in his reserved parking space in The Law Tower's interior garage. He had gotten a space near the elevators two years ago as part of his year-end bonus. He noted the cars of some of the other partners he knew. They had also come to worship at the Church of Law on this beautiful Sunday. So he could walk in the morning air, he took the elevator down to street level instead of going to crossover level three and then taking the up elevators to the firm's offices. The streets were mostly deserted.

Garnth stopped outside a small church that the downtown buildings and skyscrapers had surrounded so much that it was almost always in total shade. He heard the congregation singing "Jesus Bring Me on Home."

It's not Gospel unless you sing it.
It's not love until you bring it.
It's not faith 'til you believe in His word.

It's not good news unless you bear it.
It's not hope until you share it.
It's salvation when you say, "Yes, Jesus, Lord."

Move me, Jesus. Bring me on home.
I've left the path and been alone.
Put me on that road back home to you.
Move me, Jesus, bring me on home.
I've left the path and walked alone.
Jesus, I need that road back home to you.

I've left the straight and narrow,
Left your love that's oh so wide.

I've been a slave to sin, stood tall in my pride.
I've been dyin', but I need your livin',
Need your love and your forgivin'.
Move me, Jesus. Bring me back by your side.

It's not Gospel unless you sing it.
It's not love until you bring it.
It's not faith 'til you believe in the Word.

It's not good news unless you bear it.
It's not hope until you share it.
It's salvation when you say, "Yes, Jesus, Lord."
It's salvation when you say, "Jesus is Lord."
It's salvation when you say, "Jesus, Jesus, Lord."

Garnth walked on and passed an alleyway. Some legs with old sneakers with soles with holes in them poked out from a pile of cardboard boxes. The pile moved, and an arm rose from it. Garnth went over and grasped a dirty hand. A man emerged, disheveled, filthy, smelly, and half asleep. The man squinted up at Garnth and laughed. Garnth had felt no pain. "Took your time, Garnth," the man said.

Garnth stared for a moment in disbelief. How did this man know his name? "Do I know you?"

The man did not reply, but instead lifted the hem of his shirt and looked down at a wound below his heart. Garnth saw it. The wound began to heal. A scar formed and then faded. Simultaneously, Garnth felt a pain in his side.

The man said "Yes!" He smiled and rose from the pile of garbage. "You did know me. You do know me." He extended a grimy hand toward Garnth. "Jefferson Fuller" was all he said.

Garnth's disbelief changed into wonder as the pain in his side eased. Jefferson Lincoln Fuller, III—"JLF3"—the most famous, the most infamous, most notorious, most competent, most successful investment banker in the city; and for that matter, one of the best in the world. It was common knowledge that the acquisitions and mergers on which JLF3 worked had meant the loss of jobs for hundreds of thousands of employees. His corporate raiding included cherry picking the assets and then shutting down the companies, with jobs abolished or shifted south or offshore. The "captain of industry multi-millionaire" had been missing for over three years and now was presumed dead, possibly murdered. He had numerous enemies. The legal battle over two of his purported wills was still pending.

"I remember," Garnth said, shaking the man's hand. He felt no pain.

"Okay. Some explaining. My three years of 'public life' is up. Up when the side wound healed. And I have but one regret and many thanks."

"Three years?" asked Garnth.

"The pain, the blood, the feeling, the healing, the peace. Sometimes joy. Now it's your turn," said Jefferson.

Garnth felt his hands and feet warming, not painful. "What do you mean?"

"Don't play cute with me, Garnth. You and I have stared at each other without blinking across too many conference tables to try to fool each other now. I don't think I picked you, but He knew I thought you were one fine choice."

"Choice? Who is 'he'?"

"He's the one they whipped and crowned with pain. They made Him walk the gauntlet to Calvary, and they drove the nails into Him. He died, crucified. He's Jesus, you fool."

Garnth had never believed in anyone or anything except himself. Jesus? What he remembered from elementary school seemed like idiocy. A guy has all the power of the universe and dies naked, almost alone, stripped of all his possessions, and in agonizing pain? Senseless. "I don't believe all that," Garnth said.

"You will. You already are starting to believe. You've got wounds— hands, feet, side—don't you? Here's the deal. I've done my three years, and now it's your turn. Like it or not, you will live out these three years, and there will be pain. There will also be happiness and peace each time you take someone's pain and make it your own and he or she is healed. You will not do this voluntarily at first. Like me, you will try to hide it, ignore it, deny it, and oppose it. Then you will see. You don't know how to lay bricks, so you learn by doing what you don't know how to do—you lay bricks. Same with the pain. Same with healing. Same with love."

"Three years? No way." Garnth was adamant.

"This time your words will not affect the reality as they have done so many times before a jury. He had three years of healing others, and then His time of suffering. So will you. You are His—His new instrument. I tried to run away, tried to stop it. Then I realized this is what I was made for by Him, and this was His way of getting me back to Him. That is my one regret—I realized this way too far into my life, but not too late."

"What if I simply won't do it?"

"You do have a choice. But can you stop the bleeding? No. Can you stop the pain? No. Have you been the tool for healing someone already? I'll bet you have. You will go with this flow. One way or the other. You're free to swim with or against the current of His love."

"Now what are you going to do?"

Jefferson Lincoln Fuller III did not reply. He looked at Garnth and at his own hands, and then back at Garnth. "I don't know specifically, but I do know in general. The next right step for me is to use the gifts He has given me to get myself and hopefully some others to Him."

"Gifts?"

"Well, you probably think all these years it was all you. Valedictorian. Beat out all the other high school seniors in your city for a scholarship. You got your undergraduate As and honors. You were high school all-state and then university conference high-jump champion. Your intelligence and memory were why you aced law school. You won your first trial because you did it. You made partner early all on your own. Me, me, me! Bull. Everything that made all that possible was not of your doing. They were all gifts from Him, the one who made you. You will see. You will learn why He gifted you so much."

Garnth was incredulous, but he knew the pain was real.

JLF3 looked at him and laughed. "Yes, you are one fine choice. God bless you and keep you 'til I see you again." And then he turned and walked away down the alley.

- § -

Garnth put in his usual eleven-hour Sunday, turned out the light in his office, and closed the door. As he turned into the corridor leading to the elevator, he heard someone faintly crying. He saw a janitor's cart parked outside an office, but he saw no one anywhere in the corridor. There was someone crying in one of the offices.

Garnth kept on walking toward the elevator, but an unusual thought was trying to enter his consciousness. He ignored it. As the elevator doors closed and he pushed the lobby button, he wondered who was crying. Before he reached the lobby, he thought that the person might be in some real trouble. The elevator doors opened, and he stepped out. The lady security guard at the desk near the elevators saw him and said, "Good evening, Mr. Johnson."

Garnth nodded to her and walked back into the waiting elevator whose doors had remained open. He pushed the button for the forty-ninth floor. As the elevator rose, he shook his head, thinking, What am I doing now? He started to bleed before he exited the elevator.

As he walked into the corridor, he could still hear someone weeping. As he got closer, he knew it was a woman. He opened an office door. There was a woman, head between her hands, rocking back and forth as she cried uncontrollably. He knelt in front of her, and his pain became intense.

She looked up, and he saw her nametag, "Esperanza Garza." She jumped and started to apologize. He took her hand, and he knew. She worked two full-time jobs and then did the office cleaning on Sundays. She had three children, one of whom, her only son, had just started college. Her husband was at home, an invalid, cared for by her children and her mother. She had just gotten the notice that she was losing one of her jobs and had no hope of finding another one.

"I apologize for my Spanish," Garnth said, "but this is all going to work out." He had learned the language of Cervantes during his undergraduate year at the University of Salamanca, Spain.

Esperanza stopped crying and laughed at his Castilian pronunciation. In broken English she told him, "Señor, I believe you."

Garnth took something out of a pocket. It hurt to take a pen in his hand and write a check. He made it for twelve thousand dollars, knowing that this would cover her son's tuition for the coming semester, his books, her rent, and bills that were past due. He signed his name, and his pain started to diminish. He handed the check to Esperanza.

She began to cry again and laugh at the same time. Garnth laughed too. He told her, "This will help while you look for more work. Come back to me if your family needs more." The bleeding had stopped.

Esperanza looked at the check and became serious. Standing up, stepping back, and looking at Garnth, she said, "You are a special man. And I cannot say enough of a thank you, except to say I will pray for you. Will you pray for me and my family?"

Garnth tried to remember ever saying a prayer. He wondered, *How do you say a prayer?* "Yes," he said. Then, lawyerlike, he said, "I guess that means we have a deal—a prayer deal."

"Si, Señor Johnson," she said looking at his name on the check. "And I will see you in heaven."

Garnth hugged her and thought that no one had spoken to him about heaven for a long, long time or about his ever being there. He left the office and walked back to the elevator. He felt no pain. The holes in his skin had disappeared again, and there was no blood.

"Did you get it all done, Mr. Johnson?" the woman at the security check in desk asked him.

"Yes, thank you. I think I did ... I think I did," said Garnth as he walked toward the garage elevators.

It is, he thought, *going to be a very interesting three years.*

End Human

J esse Miltiades Carter watched the mosquitoes land on his forearm and fly away into the fog. He didn't know if it was the synflesh that held no attraction for them, the synvita fluid flowing through him, or the combination of both; but ever since he had passed being a half-half those decades ago, the mosquitoes had no interest in him. A huge dog and an even larger jaguar walked with him.

Half-half: half human, half not. The years as a drobot squad leader, platoon captain, then commander, had taken their toll, and when his left leg was replaced from the hip joint down, he had crossed over—now well more than half his body was not his. More like I'm seventy-thirty, he thought. At least I've got my brain.

"Science!" He laughed out loud at the thought. For all their science, for all their utter failures with embryonic stem cells and their stunning successes with adult stem cells, growing new ears on thigh muscle and new livers on abdominal cells, they could never make a brain. After the disasters with the embryonic cells, then the quantum leaps with adult stem cells, they thought, in their total belief in the dogmas of their religion, worshipping at the altar of the lab bench, that they could replace anything, grow anything, even make life itself. But the brain proved to be the barrier beyond which their beliefs could not take them, a dream of the high priests and priestesses of the religion of science that never came true. AI—artificial intelligence—had been promised again and again but never materialized. And, adore facts and the scientific method as they might, life, even at the smallest cellular level, was still elusive.

My brain and my thoughts are free, he mused to himself. He hummed that song from so long ago, *"Die gedanken sind frei,"* which the workers at Auschwitz had sung as they walked under the camp sign that said *"Arbeit macht frei"*: work makes one free.

Panthera, the Jaguar, and Pup, the dog, strode beside him as he saw the lights of the settlement, dimmed by the fog, some half mile away in the dense rainforest.

- § -

It was as if Panthera and Pup were littermates, but Pup had been there when Jesse had saved the hours-old cub he'd found crying next to her dead mother. It was Pup, the protective big brother, who had slept with the cub until she was over a year old. Now, when they played, Panthera, at well over two hundred pounds, rolled Pup around like a toy. Pup was like a one-hundred-thirty-pound muscle with teeth, but Panthera never hurt him.

He had found Pup, then a puppy, with an old friend in the North who bred kangals and mastiffs. "Don't know how this critter even happened—kangstiff, stiffkangal, or a mangal," his friend had told him. "And ain't never seen him like a human like he likes you." Now Pup's bite, at over seven hundred pounds, was dwarfed by Panthera's awesome, bone-cracking fifteen hundred pounds of raw jaw force.

He had trained them both to disable a supposedly invulnerable drobot by attacking silently from behind and crushing the CPU under the back of the armored neck. To Panthera it was just like a turtle shell; to Pup, a large hardboiled egg. Many times they had saved him. The Ruler's scientists, armorers, and engineers had never envisioned that such force would ever be applied to a drobot.

Jesse heard a movement high up in the canopy. He said one word to Panther and Pup: "Harp." And they froze, looking up.

He remembered those years ago when they had heard the howlers attack the eagles so high they could see nothing. As the monkeys screamed, Jesse had looked up and seen parts of a nest fall toward him—and an egg. He had caught it. It had not broken. Panthera and Pup had looked on quizzically, and Jesse knew they were wondering if they would get to share it.

Jesse had rolled it over in his palm and felt its warmth. Then he had put it in one of his vest pockets. Later that evening, he'd heard a tap-tap-tap coming from his pocket and watched an ugly downy head poking out. Again, Panthera and Pup looked on in anticipation. Jesse carefully helped the newborn eaglet from the pocket and into his hand. It did not cease the chi-chi-chi call of a nestling harpy eagle. Jesse shook his head as Panthera and Pup watched with interest. "This is our new friend," he'd said. "Not supper."

The three of them had raised Harp, a male, as if he were their own child. Jaguar, dog, and eaglet made a strange group. Soon Harp was grooming each of them with his talons, but very carefully. Of all the eagles of the continent, the talons of the harpy eagle were the largest and could exert a force of five hundred pounds. Harp was not yet full grown, but his wingspan exceeded six feet. It could reach seven. Jesse found it beyond awesome to watch Harp take prey weighing more than a dozen pounds. And he never ceased to be amazed at the family-like bonds between what should be three natural enemies.

There was a loud swooshing sound and a flutter of flashing fluid frantic whiteness from the canopy, and there was Harp at their feet. Panthera went straight to him and bent her neck. Harp cocked his head to one side and then reached up and stroked her neck with a talon. When he stopped, Panthera shook her head as if to say "Not yet," and Harp scratched her some more. Then it was Pup's turn. As if on signal, they all three started rolling around on the ground like a litter of puppies, nuzzling each other in enjoyment.

Jesse shook his head and laughed. "Strangest three musketeers I ever saw. Come on, y'all. Got some business there," he said as he pointed at the fog-covered lights ahead of them shining through the trees.

- § -

The family did not enter the settlement with Jesse. Walking down one of the dirt streets, he noticed two of the newest Trip F droidbots, the latest top-of-the-line drobots, officially known as Android Robotic Unit FFF. Jesse noted their thicker lower necks and face plates that afforded increased periphery vision.

Won't be long, he thought, *'til they have three-hundred-sixty-degree head screens*. He wondered if the family would have any problem crushing the neck and getting to the CPUs of these new ones. He did not know how soon they would be answering his question for him.

Jesse watched one of the Trip Fs scanning the street, and he knew it had captured an image of him through the fog and by now had initiated information processing.

It had been some years, but the cafe was still there. Sitting at a table near the rear wall, Jesse had a view of the entire room. Three men had surrounded one of the servers who stood with her back to a wall. At least two of them were half-halfs, or more.

"Forget it," she said.

"Now, girl, that's no way to talk to us," one of the men said as he reached out to touch her.

One of the other men pushed her against the wall.

"No!" she said vehemently.

Before any of the men could say another word, Jesse lifted one of them into the air and threw him across the room. The man's head hit the wall, and he landed, unconscious. The other two men turned toward Jesse who was now standing in front of them.

"She said no!" was all he said.

The men let the girl go and moved toward Jesse.

Something distracted him. Out of the corner of one eye, he saw the two Trip F drobots enter the cafe.

"None of your business," one of the men told Jesse as he drew a long knife from a hip scabbard. The other man was reaching for a laseblade at his waist.

With one punch, Jesse knocked out one of the men who had put on brass knuckles. The other man, now wary, backed away out of Jesse's reach. "Easy now," he said as he pulled out a knife.

"You go easy too," said Jesse as he punched the man twice and watched him slump onto a chair.

The girl crumpled, sobbing, to the floor.

One of the Trip F drobots moved behind Jesse and said, in the best artificial speech Jesse had ever heard, "Jesse Miltiades Carter, exit this structure with us now."

Jesse knew it was pointless to try to run from these machines. They could keep up with a cheetah, which was about three times as fast as the world's fastest whole human. Out in the street, the second Trip F reloaded the scan results. Jesse's visage appeared on the drobot's screen, and then the words "Human. Jesse Miltiades Carter. End Human" began flashing, superimposed on Jesse's face.

Jesse saw the young girl running out of the café to help him. She was too late. Before the drobot could begin to execute the "initiate end" command, its head snapped back. Its companion turned to look for a moment—its last moment as its own CPU was torn from its neck by Pup. Panthera sat placidly now next to the CPU from the first drobot. Pup, equally calm, moved over and sat next to Panthera. They had not made a sound. Harp flew in and sat on Jesse's shoulder.

"So, you can deal with the new model," Jesse said as he stroked Panthera's neck.

The young girl stood stock still, her eyes wide in amazement.

Panthera, Pup, and Harp watched the girl intently, never taking their eyes from her and the machete she held, waiting for a sign from Jesse. They all relaxed when Jesse said, "Thanks, little lady. Good to have backup. Name's Jesse."

The girl looked from Panthera to Pup to Harp to Jesse and then back again to Panthera. "Maria," she said. "My name is Maria."

"So, folks," Jesse said to his family, "looks like the three musketeers now have their D'Artagnan, but it's not a man with a sword, it's a lady with a machete."

"H—how do you do that?" she stammered.

"You mean my friends, my family?"

"Friends, family? They obey you."

"Yes, takes some time and a soft touch," said Jesse. "They do more than obey. They've got my back. I've got theirs. That's why they are family."

"You know this is not over. I don't know when, but this is not the end of this. More will come. Soon. The Ruler's minions will figure this out."

"I know, but I'll be safe in the forest. Even with all their tech, I can hide there. And that is why I have these friends," Jesse said motioning to his family.

"Right now, right now," she repeated for emphasis. "Let me get some food and some wine, and then you have got to hide."

Jesse paused and looked at Pup and Panthera. There was no hesitancy. "Good," he said, and then, when the girl returned, they followed her through the fog.

- § -

"Here." She had stopped in front of a hill just beyond the edge of the settlement that was actually a huge mound of what looked to be rubble and stone overgrown with vines and plants with a few trees here and there. They could not see all of it due to the fog.

"Here?" Jesse did not understand.

She walked up to one side of the mound and moved a wall of vegetation, revealing a massive wooden door. When Jesse leaned against it, it moved on squeaking ancient hinges. Maria quickly found a candle and lit it. Jesse closed the door and turned to look around at the cavernous structure, old memories coming to mind as the interior stone walls and pillars naturally brought his gaze upward.

Still looking at broken statues and faded artwork on the walls and ceiling, Jesse said, "I didn't know any of these places still stood."

"People prayed here, long ago. It would have been torn down like all the others, but for some reason, on someone's orders, the minions covered this one up, buried it. Took them months." Maria handed Jesse some more candles. "Make yourselves comfortable. This is my home now."

Maria walked to a stone slab raised near an end of the building and sat on it, taking off her sandals. She began to lie down.

Jesse knew that her bed had been an altar, the main altar in what had been a cathedral.

When, years ago, they had first detoxed his brain, flushing out decades of toxins and metals and contaminants and the mercury from all the sterilizing vaccinations and dental work, his memory had been reinvigorated. Especially after the aluminum and mercury detoxes, he noticed that he could again remember things from long ago—ten-digit numbers, peoples' names, and things that had happened last week. Now he remembered some words long forgotten as he walked toward Maria and the altar: *"In nomine Patris, et Filii, et Spiritus Sancti."* In the name of the Father and of the Son and of the Holy Spirit. He instinctively made the sign of the cross as he said the words. The whole building and the ground seemed to awaken at the words, and the earth moved ever so slightly.

Jesse continued: *"Introibo ad altare Dei."* I will enter unto the altar of God.

Now the earth quivered beneath them, the altar shook, and the family were all, instantly, apprehensive. Maria jumped from the altar, staring at it and then around the room. Panthera, Pup, and Harp were agitated, looking at Jesse for comfort.

After reciting the response, *"Ad Deum qui laetificat juventutem meum"*—to God who gives joy to my youth—Jesse stopped. The earth stood still.

He had not thought of those words from the Holy Sacrifice of the Mass for almost a century. It had, for such a long time, been called simply "the Mass," but those who planned to destroy it had, they thought, denigrated it into oblivion by calling it the "Tridentine Mass," or referring to it as "extraordinary." But it was "the Mass" that survived the worldwide evil that now held sway. The then-new so-called "Novus Ordo Mass," foisted on the faithful as "vernacular translations" complete with priestesses to preside over it, contrary to Jesus's command that only males could be ordained, had completely disappeared. For that matter, the Holy Sacrifice of the Mass was no more and had not been said on earth for a long, long time.

Maria and the family did not know what had just happened.

"They called you Jesse Miltiades," said Maria. "Who was Miltiades?"

Jesse thought back to his grandfather whose name was Miltiades and how the old man told him once that he hoped the name would be prophetic for Jesse. "What do you mean, Grandad?" Jesse had asked him. "Jesse," he had said, "we are named after a brave man who survived one of the worst, most demonic emperors and one of earth's darkest times. He lived to see the light shine again, and that is what I hope for you, my precious grandson."

"He was my Grandad," Jesse said to Maria. "I was precious to him, and he loved me."

- § -

Far, far away the Ruler, who had been questioning a man kneeling before him, paused and looked around. Then he looked out into the darkness and fog beyond his throne room. For the kneeling man this could be the moment his life ended as so many others had ended over the years.

"What?" the Ruler said out loud as he felt a tingle and then a pain in his left hand. The pain increased, spread to his right palm, and then suddenly ceased. He stared at his hands.

"Shonmak!" the Ruler screamed.

A short slender courtier hurried and knelt before the Ruler. "Your Gloriousness?" he asked timidly from bended knee.

The Ruler motioned to the kneeling man to go. He did, hurriedly. The ruler spoke to Shonmak. "Your predecessor swore to me that the last priest was exterminated over sixty years ago."

Shonmak nodded. "Yes, yes, it is so."

"No!" the Ruler bellowed. "No! Across the world somewhere, a few moments ago, the Mass was begun—by a priest!"

Shonmak did not speak for some moments. "Your Joyousness, it cannot be."

The Ruler pointed his left index finger at Shonmak's feet. Shonmak began to disintegrate, crying out in agony, "No, no, no!" No one in the throne room showed any emotion. They had seen what happened in the past to anyone who registered any apparent disagreement with the Ruler's actions.

Shonmak's life flowed away. A moment before his lips disappeared, his last words were, "There is no priest!"

"His first deputy, come forward," said the Ruler with exceeding calm.

A tall woman pushed her way through the assembled minions. She bowed and knelt before the Ruler.

"And you would be?" he asked.

"Snebin, your Goodness," she replied coldly.

The Ruler sensed something unusual. He sensed no fear in her. And real evil. He saw her five dead children. Killed at her own request. *She is,* he thought, *truly of our own nature.*

"There is a priest," he continued. "Where, precisely, I do not know, but I will because you will tell me—within the next twenty four hours."

"Yes, your Kindness," Snebin said.

- § -

It was a crime punishable by death to repeat, on any given day, any of the "titles of virtue" that applied to the Ruler. Had "Your Kindness" already have been spoken in his presence, Snebin would have died. Minions had been disintegrated for being the one to say, for the second time, "Your Goodness," "Your Unity," or "Your Truth." It took a special kind of trust when someone told another what names had already been used so he or she would not repeat them. Many an assassination had been accomplished by telling someone that a title that had already been said, had not yet been used.

Snebin had heard of true priests. She'd learned that they were hateful and to be feared, that they were always male until the Ruler's spies had infiltrated the religion and subverted it, and that they led the people astray from worship of the Ruler. She had learned that, until the infiltration of the Church by those who hated it and who served evil succeeded, there had actually been many selfless men who shepherded their people. She did know, although she had never voiced her opinion, that the Ruler seemed to become visibly upset at even the slightest mention of them. She also knew that sixty-three years ago, when the last one thought to be alive had been beheaded, the unending fog had finally covered the last bit of the inhabited earth.

She went immediately to Security Mount and addressed all who had gathered in the main assembly room: "I want to know anything that has been reported in the last week—anything anywhere that seemed the least bit anomalous, the least bit strange. Go. Now!"

Several hundred of her underlings scurried out to begin their searches. Each feared finding nothing.

- § -

Jesse thought back to that time, so long ago, and a place that had been called a "camp" in what was then called southern Florida. They had brought in an ancient man on a stretcher. He must have been over a century old, but his eyes burned like fire. When an elderly man next to the stretcher said, "This is Rene Henry," Jesse leaned over and shook his extended hand.

"My son," the old man said, "they tell me you are good. They tell me you pray."

Jesse did not know what to say.

"This is Miguel Augustin," the old man said, motioning to the elderly man standing at his side. "We are both bishops of the Church. We are both dying. I will probably go first. We do not know if there are any other bishops left anywhere or any priests for that matter. Will you consent to being ordained a priest and then consecrated a bishop?"

Jesse thought for several moments. "Then what? If I agree?"

"We do not know, but we cannot leave the world without a shepherd, a shepherd to face the world rulers of this present darkness."

"When?" Jesse asked.

"Now. Here," said the older man.

Jesse did not speak for a long time. He walked to the window. The screen was studded with dead moths, flies, and mosquitoes that had tried to penetrate it in the night seeking the light within. One bright, beautiful hummingbird had impaled itself in the mesh and died there. Yes, he did pray, and lately he prayed more and more. Finally, he thought, Why not? And then he realized that this reaction, instead of an immediate negative response, might just be God's way of calling him.

"Yes," he said as he turned back to the old men.

Where the long garment came from Jesse did not know.

"This is an alb," said Miguel Augustin. After they helped Jesse put it on, Miguel Augustin said, "And this is a stole." He placed a long garment over Jesse's left shoulder.

Rene Henry began a prayer as both laid hands on Jesse: "Almighty Father, we pray that you bestow on Jesse Miltiades, this servant of yours, the dignity of priesthood. Renew in his heart the spirit of holiness so that he may be steadfast in the priestly office received from you. May he shine in all virtues so that he will be able to give a good account of the stewardship you are entrusting to him and finally attain the reward of everlasting blessedness."

Miguel Augustin lifted the stole over Jesse's head and onto his right shoulder.

Rene Henry concluded: "O God, the source of all holiness, whose consecration is ever effective, whose blessing is ever fulfilled, pour out on this servant of yours, whom we now raise to the dignity of the priesthood, the gift of your blessing."

Miguel Augustin smiled at Jesse and told him, "Now you say 'Deo Gratias,' thanks be to God."

Jesse thought that they might be surprised to find out they did not need to translate Latin for him. Long ago he had gone two different times to a seminary, studying to be a missionary priest. Latin had become a second language to him. He said, "Deo Gratias."

The two bishops then performed the consecration of Jesse as a bishop. When it was concluded, he saw that the two men were at peace.

- § -

"Those words, those strange words," said Maria, "sounded like words spoken by my grandmother and her friends so long ago."

Jesse was curious. "The words I said? They were Latin, an old language, and they were used to pray to God for centuries."

"I have seen them."

Jesse did not understand. "Seen them? How?"

"I will show you."

Maria led Jesse and the family to the back of the old cathedral. She went to where some flat stones were laid in a cross pattern on the floor. Lifting one and then another, she exposed a plank. She lifted it away. Beneath it was a metal container, the hermetically sealed kind that was used more than a century ago to hold ammunition. It was labeled "SMALL ARMS AMMUNITION FUNC LOT TWL 82181B". A rim around its lid was sealed.

"Open it," Maria told Jesse.

Jesse pulled on the lid, loosening it. He lifted the lid and revealed a hard plastic box inside the metal box. Maria took it out and handed it to Jesse. He pushed two interlocking halves of the plastic box apart. It contained a book wrapped in flexible fabric. Unfolding the fabric, Jesse uncovered a hard cover, most likely wood, overlaid in leather embossed with a gold-colored pattern around all its edges. There were two brass side hasps that had to be released so that the book could be opened. Its spine was labeled Missale Romanum. He held it as one would hold a holy relic.

Its first page bore the words "Antverpiae ex Typographia Plantiniana MDCCXIX MDCC XIX." Jesse translated them: Antwerp by the Printer Plantin 1719." Jesse turned the first pages to one entitled "Festorum Mobilium," which he knew meant Movable Feasts, and he saw that, in the year of Our Lord 1719, the Ascension occurred on May 18 and Pentecost ten days later on May 28.

"This book is over four hundred years old," he told Maria. "I cannot believe it is here." He continued to page through the book until he got to a central section of the Mass entitled "Canon Missae," Canon of the Mass. He read out loud the words, *"Hanc igitur oblationem servitutis nostrae sed et cunctae familiae tuae, quaesumus, Domine, ut placatus accipias ."* He said to himself what the words meant: "We therefore beseech you to accept, O Lord, this offering of our worship and that of your family."

Again, the earth heaved, and Jesse's family and Maria looked around in fear until he stopped speaking and the earth was still.

Jesse closed the book, thinking about all those priests over the centuries who had opened it, and, with it open as a guide, had consecrated the bread and wine and then proceeded with the Mass, with the Body and Blood of Jesus on the altar. He said aloud from memory, "Domine, non sum dignus. Lord, I am not worthy." He thought how these words of the centurion so long ago now described him.

"My grandmother told me that it is a treasure," said Maria. "She got it from her grandmother, who got it from her mother, who got it from an old priest at a monastery in the mountains near her town. He told her to guard it. Not long after that, they came and killed all the priests—everyone there—and burned the monastery to the ground. Only this book remains."

Jesse placed the book on the altar. "We rise before dawn."

- § -

When Jesse said the word *Domine*, the pain again coursed through the Ruler's arms and hands. He held his arms out from his sides and, standing erect, shuddered until the pain was gone. Then, for the first time in centuries, he was afraid.

- § -

Snebin had analyzed a very curious report that included satellite video from a peninsula in Central Earth and records from two new drobots that had recorded something unusual but had ceased operation in the middle of transmission. A quick check told her they had not returned to their main stockade.

Whether or not this was what the Ruler wanted, it was infinitely more than nothing. In order that she could tell him that the mission was underway, before reporting back to the Ruler, she dispatched two human commanders and a platoon of drobots to the settlement. The drobots were the newest model Trip F droidbots. They would arrive right before dawn and annihilate whatever was there that was causing so much fear. The Ruler, in all his rulerness, would be pleased. She would tell him when the mission was a success.

She still could not understand the uncaring look on the man identified as Jesse Miltiades Carter as he was about to be ended in the street in front of the two Trip Fs. She wondered, *Was he smiling? Had he been ended?*

- § -

Jesse woke before dawn. He knew what he had decided to do, what he had to do. He placed two candles on the altar with some of the flatbread and the wine Maria had found. He kissed the stole, placed it over his shoulders, and then opened the book to page 235, which bore the title *"Ordo Missae,"* the Order of Mass. The Latin words of instruction were these "The priest, prepared, and having come to the altar, does the required reverence, signs himself with the sign of the cross on his forehead and on his heart, and says in a clear voice, *'In nomine Patris, et Filii, et Spiritus Sancti, Amen.'"*

Maria and the family were awakened by his words.

- § -

The Ruler, far away, was awakened by the pain. He screamed for his minions. "Get me Snebin now!"

- § -

Jesse continued with the Mass, saying the prayer before the Gospel reading: *"Munda cor meum, ac labia mea omnipotens Deus, qui labiae Isaiae Prophetae calculo mundasti ignito."* Cleanse my heart and my lips as thou didst cleanse the lips of the Prophet Isaiah with a burning coal.

- § -

Snebin walked into the throne room as the Ruler felt a searing fire in his mouth.

"What have you found out?" he yelled at her. Then he screamed to those near him, "Bring me water!" The pain was crushing him.

"Look here on this screen." Snebin pointed to one of the screens that had been set up in the throne room. "As we speak, you can see the troops I sent are beginning their assault on what we think is their hiding place." Snebin knew her life now hung by a slender thread. She had seen so many killed for so much less.

"Their hiding place?" the Ruler asked as the pain increased. "Who are they?"

Snebin replied, "An old structure in the western central continent. And it appears to be just one man, a half-half, Jesse Carter."

- § -

Panthera and Pup heard it first—the sounds of machines and drobots outside the mound. Then a bombardment of e-pulses made the mound shake. Great masses of the roof fell in around the altar. The light of a dimmed dawn began to illuminate the cathedral's interior through holes everywhere. Harp flew up and out of one of the newly created skylights.

Jesse, calm and undeterred, proceeded with the Mass. Maria moved to the base of the pedestal supporting the altar, a laseblade in one hand and her machete in the other. The whole mound had been pierced on all sides. Through holes made by the e-pulse attack, she could see drobots waiting for the entrances to be enlarged. In moments, they would be inside.

The attenuated residue of an e-pulse passing through the mound struck Panthera and crippled her, breaking her rear legs and rendering her unconscious. Pup rushed out through one of the holes and was instantly hit by a full e-pulse. His body lay on the ground, unmoving. Harp circled above.

- § -

In the throne room, the Ruler and Snebin watched real-time video feed from the assaulting force. Snebin watched, fascinated by Panthera and Pup. The Ruler was now on his knees, clutching his throat.

Jesse finished the Preface prayer and began the Canon, the central part of the Mass. As he said the words right before the Consecration, the mound was opened in three places, and the drobots poured in.

The Ruler, in agony now, watched as Jesse bent over the bread, which he had fashioned into a host. "No, no, no, no!" he screamed. The Ruler alone knew, clearly now, that it was almost over.

As dozens of drobots raised their weapons to fire at him, Jesse finished the introductory words, "... he blessed it, broke it, and gave it to his disciples, saying, accept and eat, all of you," and went on to say the words of Consecration: *"Hoc est enim corpus meum."* For this is my body.

At those words, Jesus Christ, God the Son, God Almighty, body, blood, soul and divinity, God and man, returned to earth. Jesse raised the consecrated Host high and held it there.

- § -

The Ruler collapsed. Snebin herself now staggered as she felt the sort of pain she did not know existed. Many people in the throne room had already fallen to the floor, and they were writhing in agony. Almost instantly, they were all dead.

- § -

Power radiated out from the raised and now-consecrated Host, and as the force of it touched them, the drobots crumpled into an immobile pile of black debris. The two human commanders were unconscious. A pillar of coruscating light, like a fire brighter than the sun, seemingly alive, pulsating, rose from the altar. It rose through the roof of the cathedral and shot above the mound. It passed through the fog and then spread across the sky until the entire peninsula was aglow in its brilliance. From there, the light began to branch out. As it did, minions around the world, blinded by it, dropped where they stood. The fog lifted and dissipated.

The light shone on Panthera. She stood up, shook her legs, and walked to the altar. Pup came to life and did the same. Harp flew around the mound several times. No drobot was moving. Harp flew down the pillar of light and landed next to Maria at the foot of the altar as Jesse went on with the Mass. Jesse turned and saw Maria listening to his words. She had not moved since the drobots breached the mound.

As he began the Communion rite, people from the settlement who had come to the mound approached the altar. Power and light now surrounded Jesse.

With the altar flanked by the people and sunshine streaming in, Jesse consumed the body and blood of Jesus. Then he intoned the Last Gospel from the first chapter of the Gospel of John. Its words about the true Light were not lost on him: "*In ipso vita erat, et vita erat lux hominum, et lux in tenebris lucet, et tenebrae eam non comprehenderunt ... Erat lux vera, quae illuminat omnem homninem venientem in hunc mundum*" "In Him was life, and His life was the light of men, and the light shone in the dark shadows and the darkness did not comprehend Him ... He was the true light which illuminates all men coming into the world" (John 1:1 DR).

Jesse bowed and turned around from the altar to face the people. He knew what had happened.

He raised his right hand and gave them the final blessing, "May the blessings of Almighty God, Father, Son, and Holy Spirit descend upon you and remain with you forever."

Mercy

The irony of the leg irons and handcuffs was not lost on the manacled priest as two agents escorted him down the corridor. He wore his black cassock and roman collar, and his feet were shackled together. Hobbling each half step, he shuffled trying not to stumble, putting one foot in front of the other, the chain metallically rattling on the tile floor. No one spoke.

When they came to a door, one of the agents opened it, and they silently ushered the priest into a gray room. It was cold. They motioned him to a table, attached his leg manacles to a hasp in the floor, put his hands on the table, and inserted a table-top stud through his handcuffs. Then they left.

Father Jerald Christianson, now alone, clasped his hands in prayer and then looked around the room—two mirror walls, bright lights, concrete floor. He knew why he was there, and he knew that those who had brought him there did not. He heard a door open behind him. A man and a woman walked to the other side of the table and sat down, each placing a laptop on the table. They opened them in unison and pushed the power buttons.

- § -

Behind one of the mirrored walls, Agent Willoughby, still watching the priest, asked Agent Thorpe, a man sitting at a monitor next to him, "What do you think?"

All the sensors read normal, all the electrode outputs in the table and response sensors in the restraints read normal. The retinal scanner and inspiration/exhalation monitor had found no anomalies.

Thorpe shook his head. "Can't read him. Could he have been this well trained? Who is he? Spotless record, ordained Catholic priest, good as gold, living saint. You got me. I am clueless on this one. How did he do it? How did he know? Did he do it? Did he know?"

Willoughby stared at Father Christianson through the one-way glass. "We've got nothing. He was exiled out there, miles from El Paso. Sent to the smallest armpit-of-the-world parish. Don't understand all that, but he was in the doghouse with the head guy. That's a bishop."

"What did he do?"

"They said he did things that upset this bishop. Report says things like 'standing facing the altar with the people,' 'read Romans One from the pulpit,' 'more than once, mentioned sin in his sermons. Said people could go to hell forever.'"

Willoughby was truly perplexed. "Didn't Jesus say the same things? Anyway, that's the report we got back. Doesn't sound like he got it wrong to me. I guess a bishop is a god for these guys. Go figure. Let's see how it goes."

- § -

The woman, Agent Gwen Steele, began. "Mr. Christianson, do you know why you are here?"

The priest noticed that she did not call him "Father."

Agent Robert Tilney, sitting across from Jerald, interrupted agent Steele. "Would you prefer we call you Father?"

"I am ordained, but I have no problem with any way you want to address me. If you wish, you can call me Jerry."

"Ordained?" asked Tilney. "Just men, right?"

"I have received a special sacrament that Jesus first gifted His apostles with and then the men who followed them. It is called Holy Orders, and it means that I and each man who has been ordained a priest stands *in persona Christi*—in the person of Christ. Some say they are an *alter Christus*—another Christ. And, yes, the 'only males' was a 'command of the Lord' to His Church."

Tilney continued, "Does that mean you are under orders to do this?"

"I think we are talking past each other," the priest replied.

Tilney and Steele stared at each other without speaking for a few moments.

"I don't know if ordered is the correct term. Maybe sent or commissioned is better."

Tilney asked another question: "Father Christianson, do you know why you are here?"

Jerry looked at the man and then at the woman. He thought about the answer to one of the first questions of the catechism and its answer: "Why did God make you? God made me to know love and serve Him in this world and to be happy with Him in heaven." But he didn't repeat that.

"I cannot help but think it is about what I said some weeks ago. But as to why I am here, that depends on where you are coming from and where you think you are going."

"Really?" said Steele condescendingly. She typed something on her computer and hit enter. "This is from sixteen days ago." She turned her screen to Father Christianson as a video began to play. It was Jerry speaking: "My name is Father Jerry Christianson, and I have a message for everyone. Thus says the Lord God: 'I am your God, and you are My people. I have waited so that none should perish and all would come to repentance; but I will no longer delay My promise. From the moment of your conception and for all your lives you are Mine and you are all precious to Me. The world rulers of this present darkness have led you, My precious ones, from Us, from Me, from My beloved Son, Jesus, and from the Holy Spirit. But you will not be abandoned, not a single one of you. Fourteen days from now the twelve living persons who have forsaken Me and exercised their worldly power to turn most of My children from Me—they will all return to dust. But first, before I remove them from this earth, I will give each of them a chance to repent and to turn back to Me. In twenty-eight days from these first judgments, another seventy-two will die if they do not accept the offer of My mercy. But My mercy is powerless in the face of their free will. If they freely choose not to repent, they will enter into the everlasting fire My Son told you about. In forty days, the next one thousand such people will be dealt with. In fifty days, the next one hundred thousand. And this will continue until all the evil, wicked rulers of this present darkness, and those minions faithful to them, have chosen My love and mercy, or seen My justice and power. All will see that My wrath is My mercy, and they are both My love.'"

Steele stopped the video. "That is you, isn't it?"

"Yes," said the priest.

"Who told you this? Who told you to publish it? Who are you working with? Where do you get your marching orders?"

The priest's calm complacency appeared to unnerve Steele and Tilney. Willoughby and Thorpe were speechless behind the mirrors.

"I really don't think you will believe me, but I am not working with anyone, unless you include God. He told me to do this. He gave me His message. He is the only one I am working with."

- § -

"Oh boy!" said Thorpe. "Has he been duped and used. Gotta get me some of that God Kool-Aid."

"Yes," said Willoughby, "but we have nothing on him. They have scoured his computer, his phone history, his house, his car, his parents, everywhere he went to school—pre-K through theology studies. They've read every term paper, every thesis, every transcript, every sermon anyone remembers. They've interviewed fellow seminarians and his teachers. They have squat! If he is a sleeper or an agent or a spy or an assassin, or anything, it is hidden deep. And he is very, very good at this."

"And," Thorpe continued, "what if his God did tell him all this? We only have a dozen days to stop the next round."

"His God? Wonder who that is. When the twelve were killed, he was in his parish all day." Willoughby shook his head.

- § -

Steele started a video montage on her computer. It showed the public agony and disintegration of twelve people. One was a film done by a news crew that happened to be at a press conference with a foreign cleric, a cardinal, in Holland; another video was of an interview of an old businessman in London; a third was of a woman chief executive in Manhattan. A man had confronted her and sprinkled holy water on the sidewalk. There were recordings from Beijing, Paris, Stockholm, Brussels, Moscow, Stuttgart, Chicago, Los Angeles, and San Francisco. Almost all were shot from a variety of angles from multiple cell phone captures, one after the other. They all showed bodies slowly disintegrating from the feet up, faces in anguish as they screamed in excruciating pain, the screams ending as their mouths disappeared, and the eyes wide, bulging then dissolving as each of them flowed down into a pile of black dust.

Many of the pictures ended with the dark particles being blown away. Some ended with views of a small, black pile surrounded by the shoes of onlookers, and then a gust of wind making the pile vanish. Although some of those who were vanished were easily recognized well-known persons of power, about half of them were virtually unknown to the general public.

"Were these the first dozen people targeted?" Tilney asked.

"Your question is senseless," said Jerry. "And I don't know if I would speak of God targeting His people. They are His. Their lives are His. He giveth, he taketh away. It appears that He did what He said He would do."

"So you disavow any hand in this?" asked Steele. "You say these are acts of God, not assassinations, not killings, not done by organized and very well-funded operatives or terrorists in a concerted effort with careful planning for a long time?"

"Planning? God's thoughts are not our thoughts, and eternity is not in time. I guess God must have 'planned' this forever. I think that not only are we not on the same page, we are not reading from the same book," said Jerry. "I am simply a messenger, and I have delivered the message He told me to give."

The uploaded video now had more than ten thousand times ten

thousand the number of views of any uploaded video in history. It had been translated into virtually every language around the globe.

"And it is amazing that, indeed, you did get it out to the world," said Tilney. "No news has ever gone pandemic around the world as fast as this did. And we could not shut it down. Now you are here so we can learn the truth from you, Father. And we will. But as the next deadline approaches, if you have not cooperated, we will do whatever must be done to make you tell us how to stop this."

"You cannot stop this," Jerry said placidly without emotion. "No one can stop this. I am sorry you don't understand God's power or my role, but you should know that you cannot harm me and that I am simply and only the messenger."

Steele looked at Tilney, then back at Jerry. "What do you mean?"

"I mean that I am protected. You each have a pistol. Either one of you, I am sure, could kill me with your weapon or with your bare hands. I invite you to try to shoot me or hit me. Or just try to punch me. Please."

Steele stood up and drew her pistol. She walked around the table and raised her arm as if to hit Jerry.

Tilney yelled, "What are you doing?"

Steele brought her arm down hard, but it was stopped inches from Jerry's face. Again she raised her arm and tried to hit the priest, but it was as if an invisible barrier stopped her.

- § -

Behind the mirrors, Thorpe exclaimed, "I'll be a monkey's uncle."

- § -

Steele stepped back from Jerry in disbelief as she stared first at her hand and then at Jerry. She and Tilney looked at each other, and then at the walls, speechless. They both looked at the mirrored wall as if asking Willoughby and Thorpe, "What do we do now?"

Jerry broke the silence. There was no jubilation in his voice, no joy, no irony in his manner. "You asked me if I know why I am here. I know what I have been summoned to do, and I also know what I am here to ask you." He looked up at the mirrored walls. "You are to have Jessica Miriam Clement come here to me. God wants me to speak with Jessica Miriam Clement."

Everyone except Willoughby looked blank. Only he had ever heard that name.

"Who is Jessica Miriam Clement?" asked Thorpe.

Before Willoughby could stop him, Father Christianson said, "She is your head of Trip F."

"Shut it down, now!" Willoughby yelled. "Everything off—video, sound, recorders, sensors. Off!"

"Sir?" Thorpe asked incredulously. "What's happening? Who is Jessica Miriam Clement? What is Trip F?"

"I don't know."

Steele and Tilney looked at each other and then at the mirror wall.

"Now!" Willoughby repeated.

The glow of buttons and lit screens and the buzz of equipment ceased in the rooms behind the mirror walls. Tilney and Thrope looked to the mirrored wall and then left the room.

- § -

Willoughby watched Jerry Christianson, now alone, through the glass. Jerry touched his hands together as well as he could and began to pray out loud: "Saint Michael the Archangel, defend us in battle. Be our protection against the wickedness and snares of the devil. May God rebuke him, we humbly pray, and do thou, oh prince of the heavenly host, by the power of God, cast into hell Satan and all the evil spirits who prowl about the world seeking the ruin of souls." As he finished, the room seemed to warm up.

Willoughby entered the room. This had not gone the way he had planned. For some time, he stared at the praying priest. He did not introduce himself. He reached to touch Jerry's shoulder, but his hand was stopped in midair.

"Who is Jessica Miriam Clement, and what is Trip F?"

Jerry looked up. "I do not know her, and I do not know about Trip F. But I was told to speak to her."

"And God also told you to do this?"

"Yes, before you brought me here, He told me to come here, a place I had never heard of, a place I do not know. He told me that He cares about this woman, whom I have never met." With the hint of a smile, he continued, "But He did not make it clear how I would arrive here and get to see her."

"And what is it that you are going to tell this Jessica Miriam Clement?"

"The particulars of what I am to tell her have not yet been revealed to me; but she will come. I know that."

Willoughby doubted that very much. "And what if you are simply inviting her to her death?"

"I don't know, and that may be. I don't yet know the message or the task, but I do know I am to tell her something."

Very few people worldwide knew that the FFF existed, let alone the name of its head, Jessica Miriam Clement. The agency not only oversaw all intelligence agencies—the FBI, Homeland Security, the NSA, the CIA, and all military intelligence—it also secretly and subtly directed all information gathering, collation, and analysis from almost every nation on earth. Worlwide, no new developments in computers, electronics, nanotechnology, or communications saw the light of day until FFF gave its approval.

Willoughby had heard Jessica Miriam Clement's name and the acronym FFF only by accident once when he was passing by a side office at the Pentagon. When he asked his superior about it, she had turned pale and told him, if he valued his life, to never again mention what he'd heard. Later he learned FFF stood for Fact Function Foundation, and he thought what a strange name for such a secret entity.

Now he had a decision to make about what had just happened— report what he had heard up the chain of command or remain quiet? He knew that within minutes the taped interrogation, up to the point at which he stopped it, would be going to the White House and then on to heads of multiple government agencies.

"Wait here, Father Christianson."

Jerry smiled and said, "As you wish." He held up his handcuffed hands.

- § -

Willoughby thought about what he had to do. If he hid this, his career was over. If he sent out any alerts or warnings, his career could still be over because they would ask why he had stopped the interrogation. If he acted as if he did not know about FFF and Jessica Miriam Clement, he could plead ignorance and say that he'd stopped it all since he had never heard that name.

He made his decision and went back to the control room behind the mirror walls.

"Turn it all back on," he barked to all the agents and technicians. The lights came up, the recorders were activated, screens glowed, and the computers hummed.

Willoughby returned to the interrogation room. Steele and Tilney realized something had changed. They were now spectators, and Willoughby began asking the questions.

"Tell me, Father," he said, standing across from Jerry, "you saw the videos of the assassinations. There are some notable exceptions. You said the twelve most powerful people on earth; but the president of the United States is still alive and so is the pope. What happened? Did someone not get the memo? Did someone hit the wrong target?"

"I do not know the answers. I have told you, and you must understand, that there are no targets as you mean targets. You are looking at this from a false reality. I do know that, if you pay attention to what was given to me, you will recognize that it was not simply the twelve most powerful people in the world, but the twelve who were most abusing their power and turning God's people from Him. And the same is true about the president and the pope. Maybe they are not among these twelve most powerful, or maybe they are not among the 'world rulers of this present darkness' who have done the most to hurt God's children. I did see that three people—very powerful private citizens—died and that two cardinals very close to the pope did also, one in Amsterdam and one in Stuttgart. And there was the head of the Vatican Bank. Either the president and the pope have not turned people away from God, or they have. But whatever the case, if you believe God, they were not among the twelve most powerful."

"You are saying that it may be that those who did die had power over some men perceived to be very powerful?"

"Yes. And I repeat, I spoke the truth as it was given to me to speak."

"Will the president and the pope be in the next seventy-two? Can the deaths of these people be prevented?"

"I have not been told that. I have been told the number of those who will die. I have spoken only the message, and the whole message I was given. I do not believe the deaths of these people can be prevented or stopped. You will come to know and believe you are dealing now with the power of God almighty."

"How did you spread your 'message' so far and so fast?"

"I am sure you can check this, but I posted it online as I usually do my Sunday sermon. As for 'spreading,' that was not me."

"We did check. And it appears you are telling the truth. Still, no one has ever seen anything like it."

"When is the last time you commanded the morning, told the dawn its place, taught from a whirlwind, or spoke with the voice of thunder?"

Willoughby was taken aback. "What?"

"Sorry, just remembering what God said to Job and his buddies."

"Job?"

"Yes, it is a book of the Bible, and in it, in contrition, Job says he is repenting 'in dust and ashes.'"

- § -

Less than three hours later, Willoughby was surprised to see a group marching down the corridor in full body armor, armed with rifles and pistols. They surrounded a woman who looked from side to side as she approached, hesitant, as if she did not want to be there. No one said a word to Willoughby until one of the group asked, "Where is he?"

Willoughby gestured to the door of the interrogation room. Two men entered it and looked at Jerry and then walked around the room, inspecting the walls with handheld instruments, then the floor, feeling the legs of the furniture, scrutinizing the ceiling, and once more searching Jerry. The woman waited at the door, nervous, as the other agents, three men and two women, checked out the control room and the corridor past it. Willoughby was surprised that they thought they had to check at all.

The two agents exited the room and then nodded at the woman. She entered and stood across the table from Jerry.

"You asked to see me?" she said.

"No," Jerry responded. "I asked to see Jessica Miriam Clement."

- § -

Another woman in the control room stared at the mirrored wall, silent, questioning. She removed a body armor vest and placed her rifle and pistol on a chair. She walked from the control room into the interrogation room and gestured to the woman posing as her to leave.

"I am Jessica Miriam Clement," she said to Jerry.

"I know," said Jerry.

Clement sat down and stared at Jerry, surprised that she sensed no fear in him.

"And I know who you are," said Jerry.

Clement was startled and sat upright, her eyes cold, lifeless as she tried to force her gaze to bore through Jerry. Strange, she thought, there is power here. It unnerved her. Again she tried to look Jerry in the eye, but was forced to turn away.

- § -

Jerry felt the presence of evil, and he knew that he had encountered this particular evil before. He thought back to some years ago when a Methodist pastor had asked him to come and exorcise a member of his congregation, a young girl, who lived on a ranch outside El Paso. The prayers of the pastor and his people had failed to cast out the evil from the girl. Jerry had gone to the ranch house. Outside, the temperature was 107 degrees in the shade, but inside the house was freezing cold. The girl lay spread-eagle on the floor, writhing in pain, her eyes bulging. When Jerry asked the demon its name, the demon had replied "Pacabanab and legion."

Jerry looked calmly at Clement, made the sign of the cross, and said, "Yes, I know you and, in the name of Jesus of Nazareth, Jesus God Almighty ..." As he spoke there was a physical change in Clement. Her face contorted, becoming grotesque and she began to snarl. "Jesus, Savior of all men, what is your name?" He made the sign of the cross over her.

As the name "Jesus" was said each time, and at each sign of the cross, she morphed more into a human monster, and her snarls got louder and more menacing. Jerry sat immobile, unresponsive to what was happening in front of him, unmoved by the sounds and ignoring the stench that now filled the interrogation room.

He repeated, "In the name of Jesus of Nazareth, who are you?"

In torment now, she was unable to resist. Words came from Clement's mouth as if from a caged predator: "Pacabanab ... and legion." The demonic words echoed around the room as if it was a canyon in hell.

Jerry continued. "By the living God, Father, Son and Holy Spirit," he made the sign of the cross continually toward Jessica Miriam Clement as he spoke, "I command you, serpent, and all you with it, to leave this woman and return to the everlasting fire prepared for you."

Clement's body slowly levitated from the chair and then was thrown violently around the room as she wailed and screamed.

While she was being tossed like a doll against the mirrored wall of the control room, Jerry quietly said: "I cast you out, Pacabanab, and all you unclean spirits, along with every satanic power of the enemy, every specter from hell, and all your evil companions in the name of our Lord Jesus Christ!"

He made the sign of the cross and continued to do so as he spoke. "Begone and stay far from this creature of God. For it is Jesus Christ who commands you, He who flung you headlong from the heights of heaven into the depths of hell. It is Jesus Christ who commands you, He who once stilled the sea and the wind and the storm. Hearken, therefore, and tremble in fear, you enemies of the faith, you foes of the human race, you begetters of death, you robbers of life, you corrupters of justice, child murderers, mother killers, you root of all evil and vice, seducers of men, betrayers of the nations, instigators of envy, fonts of avarice, fomenters of discord, authors of pain and sorrow. Why, then, do you stand and resist, knowing as you must that Jesus Christ the Lord brings your plans to nothing? Fear Him, and begone, then, in the name of the Father, and of Jesus Christ the Son, and of the Holy Spirit. Give place to the Holy Spirit by this sign of the holy cross of our Lord Jesus Christ, who lives and reigns with the Father and the Holy Spirit, God, forever and ever!"

The evil demons left her and flowed from the room. Her body was slumped over the table. Her face now clean, she sat up and stared at Jerry.

"Hello, Jessica Miriam Clement," he said. "I am Father Jerry Christianson." The stench was gone; the room was warm and quiet.

Willoughby watched as Jessica's face and body became clean and fresh, even glowing. He saw her look at her hands and then look up, glancing around the room as if the place was foreign to her. He saw that two agents outside the room in the corridor had fallen unconscious as Jerry prayed, and the other woman in the control room—the decoy—who had begun vomiting and writhing on the floor, was now still.

- § -

Willoughby, who had been forced up against the control room wall by an unseen force, had been released, but he could not hear what was going on. He punched and twisted buttons and switches, but there was no sound. He saw Jerry and Jessica talking, but the door to the interrogation could not be opened.

Jessica was confused. "What is happening?"

"Please hear me. I have a message for you. It is for you alone, from God, your Father."

Jessica did not laugh; neither did she rise to leave.

Jerry looked at Jessica. "You will die in twelve days. You have seen what has happened. You know you are one of the most powerful persons still living, yet you are alive. You have turned God's people from Him. God has sent you to me so I can tell you He loves you. You are to be given a chance to be truly sorry for all you have done—all of it, going back twenty-four years—and you are being given this special grace from Him. It is your choice, as it was those years ago when you welcomed the first demon and then the evil cohorts."

Jessica thought back to that first demonic blood ritual to which she had been invited in Manhattan, with the animal tortures and the child sacrifice, the politicians and the actors, the producers and the actresses, the lawyers, judges, policemen, criminals, and the doctors and nurses all taking part, and the many more ceremonies that had followed in Washington DC, Chicago, and Los Angeles. "What 'chance' if I am to die?"

"God knows the earthly power you have, the power you exercise daily, and how you have subverted and abused that power. You now have the chance to use that power to speak and spread the truth so that the world will know the message He has sent me to proclaim. You are free to choose to be His loving instrument. You are also free to choose, even now, to beseech the demons to return. If you do, you will die pitifully, and they will be with you, screaming, as they usher you into hell."

"There is not enough mercy, not enough forgiveness." She bowed her head and began to shake and weep. She had not felt so free in many years.

"This is your choice. You are free to choose. But do not doubt. Jesus died for you and your sins. Do not think there is not enough mercy, not enough love, no forgiveness," said Jerry. "If you choose, if you repent, you will have eleven days. And you will be free of the evil that you welcomed and that then held you. You are the only Jessica

Miriam Clement. Never has been one like you. Never will be another. You are free to choose to do this. No one else can do the good you choose to do. You can do this good. You can make this special Jessica Miriam Clement good come into existence. No one else."

"What am I to do?"

"You control the world's information."

She laughed. So few had known that or even suspected that Trip F existed. "But we could not stop you. Nothing worked. It was as if another power had taken over. Amazing"

"I do not mean to sound foolish or insane, but you must know that this is the power of God, God Almighty. What power you and your superiors thought you had was nothing, absolutely nothing. If you repent and if you agree, it is you who will have His message, which I will give you now, proclaimed to the ends of the earth, to all nations."

She did not deny that she could do this. This is what FFF did every day. "Message?"

"You have seen what He told me to say. It is true. I will be given more, which I will tell you. It will bring hope to those who believe. It will be the power of the sword of the Spirit, the Word of God."

Jessica paused. Then she said, "I don't know if I can say this, but I will try to do His will. His will be done."

Jerry nodded and began to tell her what had now been revealed to him, what she would add to God's message for the world.

- § -

The next morning, media around the world instantaneously presented Jessica speaking in a calm, confident, clear voice. She was seen and heard around the world via radio, television, computer and cell phone screens, speakers in public private homes, screens in bars, in airports, in restaurants, in homes, in automobiles, ships, buses, trains, and planes. Each person heard her message in his or her own language.

"Thus says the Lord God, your heavenly Father, your Brother Jesus Christ, and the Holy Spirit that enlivens and enlightens the whole world." She looked straight into the camera. Her speech was being broadcast in real time. "Repent and return to Me, My beloved children. For yet a little while now be still and trust in Me. Each of you is precious to me. I am. I am here. I am your loving God. Repent and return to Me. Choose to change your life from now on. My love for you is unlimited. For this each of you was made in Our likeness, and each of you is good. For this each of you can freely choose to make good and avoid evil. I am calling the hirelings and the wolves who have gone among you as priests, bishops, and cardinals. They cannot resist me, and they will be brought to Me by My archangels. I will deal with them. They are Mine. They will no longer lead you astray. I will send you true shepherds to lead you in the way of goodness. Repent and return to Me."

Jessica then repeated the message that Jerry had already proclaimed. She ended with these words: "Each of you, each of you one of My precious children, repent and return to Me."

- § -

The next morning when Jerry awoke, his chains fell from him and onto the floor. He knelt in his cell and thanked God for another glorious day. No one outside the cell in the corridor moved, no one said a word as he walked out. He turned a corner to see Jessica coming toward him.

Silently, for a few moments, she held his hands in hers. Then they spoke and prayed. For almost an hour, she told him her sins. Then he absolved her of all of them.

"And your Father wants you to know," said Jerry, "since you have chosen as your conscience His voice, which has spoken to you, you will see your four children whom you have never held, touched, or kissed on this earth, and you will be with them forever."

- § -

Within forty-eight hours, the world had changed. People walked everywhere, happy, openly praising God. Churches overflowed round the clock. Governments came to a standstill. As those remaining in power became more enraged, their orders to their supporters, servants, minions, and underlings became more and more frantic, with useless words ignored both by the evil ones plotting to succeed them and by the good ones who simply walked out. Some, in humility, did repent and join the crowds seeking forgiveness; but many relied on their own inner evil, thinking that, as always, it would be their salvation, that the evil ones they served would protect them from God.

Ten days later, those unrepentant ones were stunned as they began to suffer and die. Those who had come to contrition suffered, but their agony was lessened. Videos of Jessica Miriam Clement, as she disintegrated, showed a woman who suffered almost not at all, and then she smiled as her mouth moved with unheard words. Many could see that she was saying 'I love you' to some unseen persons. She was joyous.

- § -

Willoughby was still there after the twenty-eighth day had passed. He knew some of the newly dead, had worked with several of them. Some, including the pope and over a hundred cardinals and bishops, were not a surprise to him, disintegrating in anguish on worldwide television and phone screens; but so many were virtual unknowns outside the secret evil echelons of governments. Of the Vatican, and of power around the world. Willoughby was not surprised that the president still lived. Many in government recognized the profound change in him since he had taken office.

He knew what he had had seen, what he had heard. He knew if he himself was not with those of the forty days, he most certainly would be with those on the fifty-fifth day. He stood up from his desk and walked down the corridors out of the building. Entering the sunlight, he looked up and said, "Yes."

At the Shrine of the Immaculate Conception, the lines for confession spilled out into the parking lots and along the streets.

Michigan Avenue was shut down with total grid lock. Willoughby walked up to the end of one of the lines and took a rosary from his pocket.

- § -

Miles from El Paso, Father Jerry Christianson knelt in the grass outside his church and said a prayer for the repose of the soul of his bishop who had been in the last group who had died in agony.

He looked up at the West Texas sky and said, "For blessings and gifts, known and unknown, yesterday, today and tomorrow, Deo Gratias!"

Postpersons

"**D**anny said he felt sorry when they took his dad out of the home to the truck," said George. "Before they closed the doors on him, he looked at Danny and started crying."

The boys were up in the treehouse in Mike's yard.

Billy shook his head. "Then Danny shouldn't have had them come. But his dad sure did yell at him whenever he messed up. I guess he yelled one time too many."

"Danny called to ask them to bring his dad back," said George, "but they told him everything was okay now, and his dad would not be coming home."

Mike listened to it all. His own dad had been really mean lately. When he threw that wiener casserole at the wall, it made his mom get up from the table crying. "That's not fit for a father and husband," he'd said to her as she ran into the kitchen. Mike always thought wiener casserole was good—great with ketchup.

That wasn't all, Mike thought. It seemed that every day his dad found something else to get down on him about. Especially if he mowed the yard but forgot to sweep the sidewalk.

"What about your dad, Mike?" said George. "Ever think of having him PPa'd?"

"PPa" was short for "Post Person abortion." Parents deemed PPs—Post Persons—lost all rights of a legal person.

Mike did not say a thing.

"Now it's your right, you know," said Billy.

George added, "Ever since that case in court, my parents have been extra nice to me."

Right then they heard the fluctuating claxon sound of a PP truck approaching. Billy looked out.

"It's over at the Rogerson's! What has Betty done?"

The Rogerson's front door opened, and the technicians dragged a limp Mrs. Agnes Rogerson down the front steps.

"No! I've changed my mind!" Betty Rogerson wailed, clutching at her mother. The technicians ignored her. Right before they put Mrs. Rogerson into the back of the truck, she lifted her head and told Betty, "You are and will always be precious to me. I love you."

Betty screamed as two technicians held her back. "I've changed my mind!"

The doors of the truck were closing.

"Mom, I'm sorry. I love you," Betty wailed.

Mrs. Rogerson stood up straight and resisted the two technicians who were trying now to force her forward. As she said, "We will be together in heaven someday, darling," they punched her and threw her into the truck. Betty sunk silent to the sidewalk, and the windowless truck pulled away. For some moments, the boys sat in silence.

"But she said she had changed her mind," George said. "They didn't even listen to her."

When Mike got down from the tree house and went inside, he saw his dad embracing his mom. "I am so sorry," he was saying to her. Then he turned and saw Mike. "And, son, I am sorry I did that in front of you and your sisters. Sometimes I lose it and do stupid things."

Mike walked over and hugged his dad. "You are precious to me," Mike said as he hugged his father as tightly as he could, "and I love you."

Indeed Fine Wine

XXXXXXXXXXXXXXXXXXXXXXXXXXXXXXXXXXXXXXXX

Gertrude Stanley walked away from the bus labeled Cana 143 to where a scruffy man with well-worn clothes sat by a small stand. She noticed one of his eyes was closed.

"And are those real antique ancient pottery shards?" she asked him, pointing at some pieces in front of the man.

"Madam," John the Explorer replied, "you can buy all sorts of trinkets here." He gestured to the other goods arranged on tables and spread on blankets on the ground near him. "But I go to my places, where no one else goes, and I find these things. These are real. I don't go down the hill there and fill a bucket with rocks, or to some river and get water-polished stones before the buses arrive, and I don't break up made-in-China pottery so I can sell the bits to you and your friends as authentic second-century BC or third-century AD dish fragments."

"So are these from those jars that held the wine Jesus made here?" Gertrude laughed. She was referring to Jesus's first public miracle at Cana two millennia ago when He changed water into wine.

"As to their age, Madam, I cannot say, or that they are even part of an olla or an amphora, or that they held the wine of your Jesus. But I can say I found these in one of my caves between here and just across the Jordan river—my caves, no one else's."

"Let me have those four large pieces," she said, "because you are a good salesman. You might want to consider joining our church and becoming a preacher. And I guarantee you'd make more money."

John wrapped the four pieces in the plastic bags he had saved from his groceries and handed them to Gertrude. "No, this business is pretty good, and I think I will continue crawling through my caves and waiting for the Messiah," John said with a smile.

John the Explorer had always had good luck selling there in one of the several places that claimed to be the Cana of John's Gospel.

"Tell me," said the woman, "which is the real Cana?"

John the Explorer knew she was alluding to the controversy over which of several possible sites was the place of the miracle, the location of the real Cana of Galilee.

"For me, madam," replied John, "it is the location that has the largest number of scheduled tour buses that day."

"You are a true believer," said Gertrude, laughing. "Now I know it is true. The land of milk and honey is the land for those with money." With that she handed John an extra twenty-shekel note, and he thanked her.

- § -

The other vendors and merchants had nicknamed him John the Explorer because he always went alone into the wilderness and always came back with something he had found in a wadi, a riverbed, a ravine, a canyon, or a cave. He liked the area in and around Cana since he always seemed to get lucky there. And then there was the river— the Jordan River—below Tiberias, and his friends on both sides.

The Israeli soldiers were his friends and the Jordanian border guards were his friends. They all knew John the Explorer. One eye blind, lame in the left leg, and quick with a smile, he was liked by all. He was no threat to the security of either nation. He had been captured and released on both sides of the border numerous times. Often they simply let him pass and then waved him on when he returned to cross again. Occasionally they even shared a cigarette with him while they waved to their counterparts on the other side. No one cared about the rocks, pebbles, and pottery shards in his pack. If there was a newly assigned guard, the seasoned guards would be silent and smirk as John was searched by the rookie and the worthless stones and debris poured from his pack.

- § -

Herod Antipater was not happy. The soldiers had interrupted his party, dragging in a man and two large stone wine jars. Although his mansion in Tiberias was not like the palace in Jerusalem, when the drink flowed and the young women and young men danced, he did enjoy himself. To the Roman centurion leading a small procession into the banquet hall, he bellowed, "What are you doing here, Arrius Quintus?"

Bowing, Arrius said, "Your excellency, this man has been caught hiding goods from your tax collectors, hiding a large quantity of wine. He had six jars—not the small amphoras, but large stone jars, each holding much wine." Herod could see the size of the two jars. "The tax is substantial. I am told the wine is excellent. He asked that he be allowed to beg your mercy."

"And, he thinks that by interrupting my pleasure he will obtain royal mercy?" said Herod, sneering. "Have you not yourself tasted it, Arrius?"

The accused man was prostrate and had not looked up since the centurion began to speak.

"No, sire," said the centurion, "but those who have tasted it said it was the best they had ever had. And there is more to his story."

"More? You, man, stand up!" Herod addressed the accused man who looked up, trembling. "Stand up and tell me," Herod went on. "Whence comes such good wine to Tiberias?"

The centurion spoke. "Sire, actually the wine was found in Cana, some miles from here."

Herod, silent, looked at the man. The man looked around the room. "Your excellency, I did not hide any wine."

Herod yelled at the man, "What is your name? Do you know who I am? Before you address me, first tell me your name!"

The man shook even more. "My name is Simonides. We were celebrating my first son's wedding. This is my son, Zechariah," he said gesturing to a young man prostrate on the floor next to him. "It was some hours into the evening when the head steward came to me and said we were running out of wine. He did not know what to do, especially at that hour. He went away. Sometime later he returned to me, smiling, and handed me a cup of wine. I drank it. Never have I tasted such wine. My steward told me they had saved the best for last. I was so happy I did not ask any further questions."

"Really?" said Herod. "That is it? Excellent wine appears as if by a miracle, and you have no better story?" Herod could see that this man was a man of some property and that he was not lying.

"Sire," the man continued, "I was told that there was a man there, a young man. They told me he was from Nazareth, his mother a friend of the family. She told him about our embarrassment and that the wine had run out. He asked our servants to bring him some jars filled with water, and they did. He said a prayer. And the jars were instantly full of this wine. Please, your excellency," Simonides said, "we have put some of the wine into this fine olla for you personally." Simonides held up a small glazed ceramic jar decorated in beautifully colored images.

Laughter echoed through the banquet hall, but Herod was not laughing. He immediately distrusted the wine. Here was strange wine, brought into his presence from a source no one knew. "His name! What is his name?" he demanded.

"Jesus, son of Joseph, a carpenter of Nazareth."

Herod had been told this same name by several of his spies among the people. "Will you pay the fine and all the tax that is due?"

The man was silent, wondering if this was what he had to do before his execution. "Yes, sire, and immediately." He hoped his son would be spared.

Herod thought that such a fantastic story could only be true. No subject of his would chance his life for such a lie. And he had heard strange things about this Jesus. Herod turned to the centurion. "See that he does so and then let him go."

Herod looked around the banquet hall at his stunned guests. "What? Do I not know mercy?" He looked back at Simonides. "But leave this wine here!"

Simonides was dumbfounded. He backed away from the king, "thank you" after "thank you" falling from his lips.

Herod spoke to all there: "Leave, all of you, except you Arrius Quintus, and you," he said, pointing to Demetrius, a young man who had been dancing. "And you." He pointed to Simonides's son, Zechariah. "Bring me the small jar," Herod said to one of the servants, "and three cups." When this was done, Herod ordered the servant, "Now pour three cups." The servant carefully did as he was told. Then he offered the first cup to Herod. "No, no, no!" Herod said vehemently without touching the cup. He dismissed the servant. "Arrius," he said almost pleasantly, "this is for you. Tell me if it truly is the best wine."

- § -

Arrius Quintus was no one's fool. He had not become a centurion by taking senseless risks, but his bravery in battle bordered on the foolish. Without the slightest hesitation, he said, "Thank you, your highness." And he took the cup and drank the wine. If this was to be his end, so be it. At least he would die doing his duty. He had never tasted such wine in his life, not in Judea, not in Greece, not in Gaul, and not even in Rome. And it had some curious warming effect on his whole body. He did not know what he was feeling.

Herod stared at him intently. Then said one word: "Arrius?"

The centurion put the cup down. "Indeed, this is fine wine, sire. Indeed."

Herod gestured to Demetrius. Smiling, Demetrius took a cup and downed the wine quickly. For a few moments, he looked blankly ahead. But then he pitched headlong to the floor, dead before his quivering body rolled over, eyes wide open, staring at the ceiling. For a moment, Herod thought about Demetrius, whose crimes and debaucheries he knew too well.

Herod watched this with no visible emotion or reaction. Then he looked at Zechariah and pointed to the third and last cup. Zechariah's hand was shaking as he took it. "Come, come, young man, have you not already had your share of this fine wine?" Herod asked tauntingly.

"Yes, your excellency," Zechariah said as, his hand shaking, he put the cup to his lips and drank its contents. He moved the cup away, looked at Herod, and then smiled. "It is fine wine indeed, sire, fine wine." Never was a person's relief more evident.

"Tell that to Demetrius," Herod said, looking down at the dead man. Such a handsome young man, he thought. Herod was perplexed. Fine wine or not, it was surely strange wine. "You leave, now," Herod said to Zechariah, "but not you, Arrius Quintus."

Arrius stood alone next to the corpse of Demetrius.

"Arrius, you are a trusted soldier," said Herod. "Take all the wine—all the large jars and this small one. Go to the river, to a deep part, and throw it all in—all of it. Get rid of all the jars. Tell no one what you have done or where you have gone."

"Yes, your excellency. I will go now."

Herod had already heard of this Jesus of Nazareth, and now he feared him. "And come back here to me in the morning."

- § -

It was a moonlit night and fairly easy going in the darkness down to the river Jordan. Two soldiers each carried a large jar, and Arrius carried the smaller one.

"Is this that deep spot, Cornelius?" Arrius asked one of the men.

"Just a little down from here, sir. There, you can see the curve in the moonlight. The inner side of that curve," said Cornelius.

After scratching some words into the jars, Arrius addressed the soldiers. "Throw these two jars in here." Arrius pointed with his sword when they had arrived at the curve in the river. "Now, go back to the barracks and get some sleep. I will follow later."

The two stone jars made loud splashes as they hit the water, floated for a moment, and then sank below the surface. The soldiers turned away and began walking back to Tiberias.

Arrius watched them. He knew what he was going to do. He did not understand, but he knew. With the point of his sword, he etched the same words into the small jar in Latin, in Hebrew, and in Greek:

"Jesus Wine Cana." Then, after ensuring that the jar's seal was in place, he took off his centurion's helmet, placed the jar in it, and threw them into the river. After removing his cloak, he wrapped his sword in it and threw it too into the water. Then he took off his armor and his boots and his outer garments and tossed them as far as he could. In the moonlight, he looked to the heavens, and walked in the direction of the flowing river. He was never seen again by any Roman soldier in Tiberias or by any member of the royal court.

- § -

"Good hunting," said one of the Israeli guards as John the Explorer trudged off down to the Jordan river. "Which side will you pillage tonight?" Another encouraged him, "Make sure you take it all from the Jordanians and leave the gold of Solomon alone." All the guards present joined in laughter.

John replied, "You know I cannot divulge where the treasure is buried. Shalom 'til next time."

John walked along the edge of the water. Because of the recent lack of rain, the river was down, and in the moonlight, John could see stones and formations exposed that he had not seen for a long time. He thought that the tourists would be buying some very pretty polished rocks if his friends would only come here to gather them.

At a curve in the river, he thought he saw a glittering light from beneath the water. As he walked closer, something glistened and sparkled brightly. Reaching down into the water to grasp whatever it was, at first he missed it. The water's refraction and his one-eyed depth perception fooled him. Trying again, with his arm in water up to his shoulder, he felt a blade. Holding on to it, he lifted it up. The blade, less than a meter long, sharp on both sides, was that of a sword. With its hilt, when he held it up, it cast a shadow cross on the water. Looking at the cross, he saw there was something else submerged that was reflecting the moonlight.

John had to go under the water to retrieve this other object. He tried to pick it up, but it was embedded in the river bottom. He surfaced without it and then went under again. After loosening soil around the object, and after several more tries, he freed it and rose from the water holding a helmet with something inside.

"God be praised," he said to himself as he walked to the bank where he had laid the sword. "Amazing," he said out loud. He cleaned the helmet and rinsed it in the river. It was incredibly well preserved. The object inside proved to be a small jar.

John took the jar to the water's edge and cleaned it too. He knew the Hebrew and then guessed the other writings: "Jesus Wine Cana." He thought to himself, *This is one fine joke.* All three items—the sword, the helmet, and the jar—were pristine, as if they had never been submerged in the Jordan.

John placed them on a large stone, lined up in the moonlight. Then he saw that the jar had a seal. He picked up the jar. At first, he thought he was hearing the flowing river, but then he realized he heard liquid sloshing around in the jar. He looked up at the stars and laughed out loud. "A fine joke, truly!" He wondered if some pranksters were at that moment watching him. But for the sounds of the river, the night was quiet.

Peering at the jar, John took out a small knife and tried to unseal the stopper that closed off its opening. It was held solidly in place. John worked at it, carefully, and eventually loosened it. Expecting to smell some rancid rotten liquid, he held the jar to his nose. "Truly amazing," he said to himself as he smelled wine. "This is one very good trick."

"Well done!" he yelled to the darkness, to the unseen jokers. There was no reply. After smelling the jar's contents one more time, without thinking of any risks, John put the jar to his mouth and drank. He immediately felt as if the wine flowing in him was enlivening his whole body. His blind left eye began to burn, and his lame left leg pulsated. John set the jar down and sat on a large rock, looking around to see if the ones who had done this, and probably drugged the wine, were going to dance around ridiculing him. But the night was again quiet. And John stood up.

He rose easily on both legs, feeling as he had not felt since he was young. He did not fall. Instinctively, he held both arms out for balance, his cruciform body casting another shadow cross on the flowing water. He stood stable and solid at the river's edge. Then he looked at his hands—with both eyes. Closing his right eye, he held both his hands before him in the moonlight and counted his fingers. He had no thoughts, only wonder.

He looked to the heavens and said, "This, Jesus winemaker, is indeed fine wine."

- § -

Professor Abraham Ben Joseph sat at his desk and held the small alabaster figurine in his hand. Rays of the morning sun played off it as he ran his fingers over its smooth surfaces. He thought to himself, *Ten in the morning and I am enjoying this thing of beauty, this work of art that is millennia old, and I do not have to rush off to some meeting at which competing academics would have an internecine battle over how some grant money was to be spent, whose name would go first on a journal article, or who would get to use some small few square feet of office space.* Since he had resigned from the department chairmanship, he could return to his first love, archaeological research and field work.

He thought about the artisan centuries ago working on the figurine and then presenting it to someone, perhaps a rich woman or a political leader, or a child. He imagined the recipients' pleasure at the fine work. Then he looked up to the doorway to his office to see a figure standing there, a figure familiar but strange. "John?" he asked.

"It is me, Abraham," said John the Explorer as he walked easily, without shuffling, into the office carrying a large canvas bag. Abraham simply stared and said nothing as John sat down in a chair by the desk.

"You walk," said Abraham.

"I walk and I see."

It was only then that Abraham looked at John's eyes and noticed that the left eye was not closed and appeared healthy. "How?" was all that he said.

"You and I have shared a great many things, Abraham, and I know that, joke as we might, we share faith."

Abraham looked puzzled. Something very strange had happened and was happening.

John continued. "Telling you will not convince you so much as showing you." With that John opened the bag and carefully placed the sword, the helmet, and then the small jar on the desk." Abraham's amazement increased as each object was removed from the bag.

"Listen," said John. He picked the jar up and moved it from side to side. Abraham heard the liquid and, as John replaced it on the desk, saw the writing: "Jesus Cana Wine."

Abraham covered his mouth with his right hand as he spoke the words, "Oh, my God. Can I touch them?" John nodded.

Abraham took the helmet first and held it up, turning it over and over in his hands. "Definitely an officer. Definitely first century AD. Probably a centurion."

Abraham used the AD abbreviation to rebel and to upset his colleagues who had religiously converted to the secular religion's new "CE." He liked that the *Domini* of the AD was Jesus, the Messiah of the Jews and the Son of God of the Christians. And the irony was not lost on him of the new pagans thinking they could deny this Messiah by using CE and BCE. They thought of these as "current era" and "before the current era," but, of course, they meant the "Christian Era," and "Before the Christian Era." And then, as he looked again, holding the helmet out from him, he said "And definitely real."

Then he held the sword, carefully because of the double opposed razor-sharp edges. "Real. The best Roman short sword I have ever seen—or heard of," he added. Abraham could not make sense of the condition of these things, their evident antiquity, and the fact that was clear to him that they were real.

He then put his hands around the jar and raised it from the desk. He heard the liquid inside and looked at John, questioning.

"Yes," said John, "I drank of it." Abraham tilted his head as if to ask for more. "And, yes," John continued, "then I could see and then I could stand and walk."

Abraham knew instantly the value beyond value of what John had discovered. "Your days of crawling through caves and sneaking over borders are over, my friend. God Himself can now dismiss this servant in peace because you have shared these things with me. What will you do?"

"I don't know. That is why I am here with you. You have always been good to me. You have never laughed or ridiculed me, and you are the most honest man I know. You tell me."

Abraham thought. There were infinitely more scoundrels than good men involved in the trade of such objects worldwide. "I know one man. He is with Sallsbary Antiquities Global. Gary Lamont. He is in Jerusalem. Him you can trust. It would be my great pleasure to meet him with you and show these to him. It would be my real pleasure to see him touch them for the first time."

- § -

At first Gary Lamont was incredulous, but then as he examined the three items and could see that they were not counterfeits, he knew that, whatever the story was, they were real. "Never have I seen or heard of things like these in this condition. Never." He touched the small jar and ran his fingers over the inscriptions. "Forget for the moment the inscriptions. Even without them, these things are priceless, beyond value. Not only every collector, but many governments will want them, and probably will claim them, even not knowing their source."

Abraham spoke for John. "And being what they are, your usual terms will be thrown out the window. And John here will be a very happy man."

"Yes," Gary replied, "and my reward will be being known as the one who helped John."

- § -

It was the night before the auction at Sallsbary Antiquities Global's London show room. The moonlight reflected off the glass face of its north side as four men silently descended on cables down from the roof. Their movements were mechanical, precise, with no wasted effort. Once they made their way through a pane of glass that an accomplice had carefully removed and set to the side, each did his task of disabling alarms, checking for movement, and countering warning systems. One periodically emitted a nitrogen fog from a canister of the liquid on his back and then held a temperature sensor in front of him.

Once they got into the room where the helmet, sword, and small jar were displayed, each under its own glass dome, one of the men produced an infrared laser, focused it on the dome above the jar, and waited a few seconds. He gestured to one of the men, who wore insulating gloves, to raise the dome. A third man removed the jar and deposited a duplicate jar in its place. The dome was lowered over the counterfeit jar.

As quickly and silently as they had entered, the men left, replaced the glass pane, and climbed up to the roof. Then they were gone.

One of the men, clearly the leader, spoke into a cellphone. "We have it. We are one our way."

A voice from the phone, with no noticeable accent, said, "Good. Go to Stansted airport. There is a plane waiting. Tell the pilot to take the southern route. He'll know what that means. You fly down along the coast of Africa and then release the wine from the plane after you turn inland at Rabat. One vial is to be kept—one vial only—which you bring to me, to no one else. Do you have the vial?"

"Yes," said the man holding the jar. The call ended.

- § -

John sat in the last row in the Sallsbary show room. It was an hour and a half before the auction was to begin. He saw a security detail bring in his treasures and place them on pedestals near a podium. Then he saw Gary Lamont enter, followed by two men surrounded by security officers, each of them talking loudly and vehemently gesticulating, evidently unhappy with something. Gary Lamont looked at them, held up his hand to silence them, said a few words, and then turned and walked away from them.

Getting up and moving to the front of the room, John thought about all those years, all those times he had searched through the caves in the darkness, all the things he had found. Standing before the pedestals, he smiled to think how far he was from Cana.

"They are dreams, aren't they?" Gary said.

John turned around. "Yes, and in some ways, I wish I was back there in my caves."

"Those men who were just here would dearly like to speak with you. One represents the Israeli government and the other is from Jordan. They each claim these things for their governments on the basis that you found them."

"And," said John, "no one but I know where they came from. Odd that no one else has claimed them."

"That is not exactly true," Gary replied. "We have a communication from a monsignor at the Vatican Archives. They have made a not too subtle request to receive a sample of the liquid for testing and for carbon dating and, he said, if indeed it is from that time so long ago, the Church may make a claim to ownership of the wine. What was Christ's they believe to be theirs."

John laughed out loud, shaking his head. "They must have a holographic will, signed by the bridegroom to whom Jesus gave the wine. He must have been one of the first Catholics."

John glanced at the small jar and then focused on it under its clear dome. He looked at it and looked again. Something was odd. He walked around the pedestal that supported it, and then he glanced over at the helmet and the sword. It was only the jar. It was not right. He knew the colors and the decorations. Two designs were wrong, and they were colored wrong.

Gary said, "what are you looking at?"

"Come here," John said, as he continued to stare at the small jar. "This is not the jar I found."

An hour later, the auction proceeded, but only for the helmet and the sword. The announcement that the jar had been withdrawn, without explanation, brought groans from all the assembled bidders.

- § -

"Sir," the pilot said to the man in the suit who was the only passenger, "in ten minutes we will head inland over Rabat and then on across the Sahara as directed to Ajdablya."

"Noted," said the man with no sign of emotion as he rose to go to the lavatory. The toilet had been reconfigured as he had directed.

Carefully, he filled three vials with the wine, noting that it still smelled like new wine. Then he poured the rest into the toilet and flushed. The wine did not vaporize. Remaining intact, a shower of red droplets fell on the desert below.

The first droplet to hit glistened on the surface and then oozed beneath the sand. In moments, water rose from where it had entered the sand, and then a stream began to gurgle up and flow down the dunes. And so it was for each droplet as the cloud of wine flowed over the entire Sahara and into the Middle East.

The man, unaware of what was happening beneath him, placed a call. "Yes, it is gone. Yes, I have the vial. Yes, only one vial. "I will arrive in the morning."

- § -

For all his nineteen years, Abdelah had known only the Moroccan mountains and desert to the east. His family had farms of many acres, but many acres were required to raise even one goat. He wanted to change all that. His studies told him that the existing water supplies could be used more effectively and that new technologies could make Morocco's desert regions and the semi-arid regions to the west of the Sahara, between it and the mountains, good arable land that could be used for productive agriculture. The ancient stories and legends spoke of an ocean under the sand. He knew it was there.

He had set out before dawn. As he came to the top of some large dunes, he saw the light from the sun on the horizon playing tricks on him. There was what appeared to be a small rivulet, a stream of water flowing up from the sand. Small bits of green foliage had sprung up along its edges, and one blooming flower. He stared. Then he bent down and put his hand in the water. Rising up, he turned his hand over and over as the water fell back to the earth. He tasted it. Pure water. Water!

It was the same across the entire Sahara going south and going east and all the way to and past Saudi Arabia. Water. Foliage. Water. Grass. Flowers. Water!

- § -

The man in the suit approached the guarded doorway, an armed man walking on each side of him. One guard nodded and opened the door. Within the room there were two more guards one on each side of the doorway.

"You are safe, Miguel, and you are here!" said the voice from the phone call. A man sitting on a sofa gestured for Miguel, the man in the suit, to sit in a chair across from him. "You and the wine have had a long strange journey to get here."

"Yes, sir," was all Miguel said as he handed a single vial over to the man on the sofa.

The man called out, "William! Bring two cups." A young man, who could have been no more than twenty years old, walked in from an adjoining room carrying two small cups.

The man emptied the contents of the vial into the cups. He handed one to William and held one himself. "Have you heard about this wine?" he asked. "It is life for you and me." With that he gestured, as in making a toast. William did the same, and they both consumed the wine. Miguel watched, stone-faced, unmoving.

In moments the man and William were dead in their seats, their bodies still quivering, their faces frozen, showing no emotion—no horror, no amazement, no shock. Nothing except stone cold death.

Miguel rose and walked to the door. One guard looked fearfully at the other. Neither of them made any attempt to stop him. Miguel walked out of the mansion and, as he got back into the rented Mercedes, he grasped the two vials still in his pocket. "Strange wine, indeed," he said out loud. As he drove away from the compound, he wondered where exactly the wine had been found, and if there was more. He was certain he would find answers to his question.

- § -

"Scientists and climatologists are scrambling, but the most common word used for what is happening across north Africa and the Middle East is *miracle*," said the BBC announcer as the screen showed one satellite photo after another of verdant land, flowing water, flourishing plants, and the leaves of small trees blowing in breezes. Last month, such greenery had been nonexistent in the sand and heat. "Michael Trollope of the International Climate Agency in Brussels has stated with assurance that the theory of anthropogenic global warming can be, in his word, 'tweaked' to account for this phenomenon, unprecedented in our lifetime. He adds that climate change, now more recently renamed 'climate catastrophe' for political purposes, is still a problem that can be solved only by empowering a world-encompassing agency to take control of everyday life."

John the Explorer, half listening to the news as he read a paper, looked up from his seat in the departure area. He was waiting to board a flight to Frankfurt that connected to an El Al flight to Tel Aviv. The more he listened, the more he wondered, *Is there some connection? The missing wine container, the wine, the desert miracles?*

The news commentator on the monitor near John was reporting on messages from leaders of at least five countries changed by the climate 'miracle' and pleas from these leaders to their citizens who had left, the majority going to countries in Europe. The miracle meant that the economies of these countries would change overnight. And workers of every kind were needed.

"Now boarding all first-class passengers," sounded over the speaker system. John picked up his carryon. A chrome railing sparkling in the sun made him think of the two shiny smooth and rounded surfaces he had seen beneath the Jordan river, two things that were still there. Two things he would go back for. Two treasures he would find. Indeed, it was fine wine.

Ranger

"Seven dead—that we know of. No pattern except all victims had Jell-O for brains. Nothing but dead ends." DCI Shope of Her Majesty's Territorial Police Force, Surrey Region, south of London, was not happy. He slammed a file down on his desk. "And this is down to me."

George Leddemer, youngest detective sergeant at the station, tried to console him. "It will break. There is a fact, a clue, a trail, a connection, something."

"We have the facts, and more facts, evidence and more evidence, and more reports. Facts, facts, facts, and no suspect," said Shope despairingly.

"We need that guy from Texas. They called him the human computer. He not only remembered it all, he could put it all together. I think his name was Menger."

Shope, incredulous, was shaking his head. Leddemer's head was filled with useless trivia. "Menger? Texas? What are you talking about?"

"It was some time ago—years ago. He's probably dead by now. Genius bloke—photographic, video, eidetic memory. Texas Ranger. And his wife was murdered, in her fifties, before she could die from lung cancer she'd just been diagnosed with."

"So? You're going to get him to come here to England to help us?"

"So she had terminal cancer, a few months to live, and was killed anyway."

Shope nodded. "Now I see where you're going." All our seven victims—men and women—had cancer. Ages forty-four to sixty-seven, all terminal. "What do we have here, an angel of death?"

"This would be a devil of death," said Leddemer. "That's why I said Menger. He put it all together. He saw the big picture, literally. With that memory, he tracked down that demon."

"You'd think," said Shope, "with all these high-tech cameras and computers we could do that—pull it all together."

"But," said Leddemer, "you need to know the right questions to ask the machines. You need to think outside the computer paradigm. That's why you and I will always have a job. That and the fact that they can't make a pill to make people good or make a computer that thinks, or tells a joke another computer laughs at, or one romantic computer that passionately loves another."

"Well," said Shope, "you just sort it out on your vacation. Where are you going?"

"Got nothing planned yet. Probably stay here and read a good spy novel."

"Or," said Shope, laughing, "knowing you, you'll read the phone book in the morning and the nineteen-eighty-seven almanac in the afternoon." Shope never could understand George's penchant for minutiae, weird facts, and worthless knowledge. He remembered George telling him Jane Austen wrote *The History of England* and called Elizabeth I a disgrace to humanity, a pest of society, and a murderess. Once George put this trivia in his brain, he could not get it out. Who cared?

- § -

When you read about the heat and humidity in Texas and see news reports with people walking around in their usual routines in short-sleeved shirts, it simply does not convey what Leddemer felt when he had gotten his luggage from the carousel and walked outside into a June in Houston.

So this is Hades, he thought. The blast was like walking into a human-sized convection oven. Skies clear, temperature ninety-seven, and humidity ninety-five at eleven in the morning! And smoke billowing up from all the travelers lined up outside along the terminal, the ones who had not had a cigarette for hours, as if the Texas sun had ignited each one of them.

When he had searched for John Menger on the net, to his amazement, he found that Ranger Menger was, apparently, still alive. A last-minute ticket on AirEasy to San Antonio, round trip, on sale, was $370. A stop in Houston. So here he was. His connecting flight to the Alamo City would leave in forty-five minutes. The man in the seat next to him had told him that Houston would not exist if air conditioning had not been invented. George, beginning to simmer in the heat, realized this was not a joke.

John Menger had a post office box address in Comfort, Texas. George thought, *How could there be any comfort in Texas?* But the navigation voice in the rental car assured him, as he drove out of the rental lot at San Antonio International Airport, he would be there in fifty-six minutes. Outside, the temperature was ninety-eight. "Thank heaven for A/C," he said out loud.

United States Postal Service Comfort, Texas, the sign informed him. George asked the man behind the counter, "Hello, can you tell me the way to John Menger's house?"

The clerk behind the counter looked at George quizzically. "You're not from around here, are you, son?"

George laughed. "No sir, and we don't have heat like this where I'm from."

"Heat?" the clerk asked. "Son, this is gentle. Next month it'll get hotter than the brass hinges of the gates of Hades, and this will feel like a cooler. How can I help you?"

"I am looking for a man named John Menger."

"Yes, he lives in these parts, but it's against regulations for me to tell you where."

"But he has a P.O. box here," argued George.

"That he does. Still, I am not authorized to give out his home address. Why do you need to see John Menger?"

George took out his badge. "I am with Her Majesty's Police Force," said George, "in England, and we were hoping he could help us with a matter we are investigating."

"I see. 'Her Majesty.' No, can't tell you where he lives. Is this your first time here?"

"Yes. I've never been in Texas before."

"Well, if you were looking for some beautiful views, my advice would be to go down Highway twenty-seven and turn left onto Hermann Sons Road. Go down about three miles. Real pretty this time of year."

"I might just do that, sir. And you have my thanks." The clerk smiled and went back to his work.

George made the mistake of touching the steering wheel before he turned the A/C on. After waiting a few minutes until some "cool" air—air below a hundred degrees Fahrenheit—started flowing, he pulled out of the parking lot with the navigation advising him: "U turn, one hundred yards, U turn now, to U.S. Postal Service". George pushed the cancel icon.

It was country like George had never seen, so unlike the country around his home. A roadrunner raced down his side of the road, cut across in front of him, and then stood stock still. George never knew that the roadrunner Wylie Coyote chased was so beautifully multi-colored. He saw a license plate that said "Texas God's Country," and he wondered if there really was a God. He now knew there was a Hades down below. Cresting one hill, he stopped and looked off into the distance. He could see over twenty miles to the horizon. In three places he saw thunderstorms with lightning hitting the ground. There was blue sky between them. "Beautiful!" George said out loud.

The label on the rusted mailbox said "J. Menger." George stopped his car at the gate. Down the hill through the brush he could see a structure that was more like a cabin than a house. A dog started barking. George heard an engine start and then he saw what looked like an antique Nazi command car from World War II leave the cabin and head toward the gate. As it got closer, he could see it was actually the better part of two such command cars melded together end-to-end. Sweet ride, he thought.

Before the vehicle stopped, the dog, a blue tick hound, was out, running to the gate, and barking, announcing that George was unknown. A tall man with a full head of gray hair got out of the vehicle and looked at George for a few moments. Then he walked toward the gate. The man said one word, softly—"Down"—and the dog was silent.

"What can I do for you, son?" The voice was calm, serene.

George stepped out of the car. "Sir, my name is George Leddemer. I am with Her Majesty's Police in Caterham, Surrey, England, near London. And I would like to speak with John Menger."

John stared for a few moments before replying. "Her Majesty? About what?" he said laconically.

Funny, George thought, he said 'Her Majesty' almost as if he knows the queen personally. George was certain this was John Menger. He looked like the photo on the internet, only some years older. "We have a case, sir, and I was hoping I could ask you to help us with it."

No smile crossed John's face. His stare was unchanging. He seemed deep in thought. George did not know what to say.

"Son, I am John Menger." He reached his hand out to George over the gate. John was six feet four inches tall, and his hands were sized in proportion to his height.

Strong handshake, George thought. "It is very good to meet you." But John made no move to open the gate and asked no more questions.

"Son, you've come a long way to talk to a man who does not do that anymore. My ranger days are done. Right now, today, there are a million bad fellas out there who did bad things yesterday. They are going to do them again today, and tomorrow there will be a million more. Now I wake up in the morning—actually the mockingbirds wake me up singing—and I am not thinking about anyone's death, any crimes, any motives, any clues, any facts or data or files or papers. And me and that dog over there, we laugh a lot."

"We've got a serial killer, sir," said George, "going back at least two years, probably more, and there are seven dead we know of. And no one, not even New Scotland Yard with all their computers and high-tech resources has a lead of any kind. And I thought of you."

"Me?"

"Yes, sir. I'm kind of a trivia nut."

"And you found me in that trivia?" John smiled for the first time.

"Well, sir, yes, sir. They smile like you do—my boss, DCI Shope, and the rest of them. Laugh at my 'useless facts.' But I remembered that, some years back, you solved a case like ours."

"DCI—detective chief inspector. Now there's a rank I haven't heard in some time," said John. "Some years back I helped out some old friends in the Yard." He did not tell the young man that, indeed, he did know the queen personally. "There's more cases than fire ants. No matter how many you kill, they are always here, always. I am sorry, son, you've come a long way. I thank you for remembering me, but I don't think you can match my wake-up songs. I hate to disappoint, but for me, it's over."

"I knew that would probably be how this turned out, sir, but I had some time off, the case has gone cold, and somehow I ended up in San Antonio. Can I give you my card so, if you change your mind, you can get in touch with me?" George offered John one of his cards.

John looked at the card, then took it. He read from the card, "Sergeant George Leddemer. Email gleddemer-each-hmpf period org period uk."

"That's not 'each'," George corrected him. "That's an email address. It's not 'each'; it's 'at'."

Still staring at the card, John said "I see. Well, young man, good to meet you and good luck."

George opened the door to his car but stopped before he got in. "I said 'a case like one of yours.' There was something all the cases had in common."

John moved to get into his command car.

"All kinds of victims," George went on, "men, women, old, young. But all had terminal cancer."

John stopped and paused, and the slowly turned around. He stared, unmoving. He looked down at the road. Then he looked up. George was not sure, but it looked like a tear in John's eyes. "You said you are working with New Scotland Yard. With whom?"

"Old bloke," said George, catching himself before he had also said "like you." His name is Superintendent Geoffrey Argyle."

John chuckled. "Do you have one of those new phones with you, son?"

"Yes, sir." George took his cellphone out of a pocket.

"Can you call across the pond with that? Can you get this superintendent on that thing?"

"I can try, sir." George checked to see if he had a signal, then pulled up his contacts list and pushed a button.

"Tell him my name," said John Menger.

"Yes, Superintendent Argyle please. Yes, I know it's gone half eight there. It's Sergeant George Leddemer, but please tell him I'm in Texas with a man named John Menger."

- § -

It had been some time since Ranger Captain John Menger, retired, had been on an airplane, and the coach seat did not fit his tall frame very well. As he sipped his coffee, he was deep in thought.

George was trying to fall asleep in the seat next to him. Every now and then George thought about the phone call between John Menger and Superintendent Argyle, back at John's place in Comfort. John had listened with the phone's speaker on.

"This is Superintendent Argyle."

"Sir, this is Detective Sergeant George Leddemer out of the Caterham station, and I'm here in Texas with a man named John Menger. We're on speaker, sir."

There was a pause. "Did you say Texas?"

"Yes, sir."

"And did you say the name 'John Menger'?"

"Yes, sir."

Both George and John could hear a deep belly laugh.

"John, it has been some time. Too long."

George watched and listened in amazement.

John did not know if he had to be holding the cellphone, but George motioned that it was okay. "Geoff, how have you been?"

"Been well, John. I heard about your wife and want you to know how sorry I am."

"She is in a better place, and you and I should hope to be there with her someday."

"John, how are you doing?"

"On the right side of dirt, and my dog still loves me," John said.

"I cannot believe, after fifteen years, we are talking again. And I can't believe one of ours is in Texas with you."

"Bright lad you have here, Geoff," said John, glancing over at George. "He's told me about a case y'all have—seven victims, nothing to go on, but they all had terminal cancer."

"We're flummoxed, John. Actually, now we know of eight victims. One more since George left."

"There you go like always with those three-dollar words, Geoff. You can use some nickel and dime words and I'll understand. So by flummoxed you mean like a dizzy goat on astroturf, and y'all are looking for your butts with a flashlight in both hands and still searching?"

George suppressed his laughter, but Geoff did not. He laughed out loud. "John, we've run out of batteries."

"George said y'all could use some help. I've got two conditions. One, I do not like to be wet or cold."

"Got your umbrella right here, John, and I can get you some extra blankets even though we are having a lovely summer here. What's number two?"

"This young man here works with me, kind of like he is detailed to me."

George smiled. He took this as a complement.

"Does this mean you will actually fly across the pond?" Argyle asked.

"Yes, sir, superintendent, and I will do what I can."

- § -

Waiting in the line for customs at Heathrow, George asked John if he wanted to go straight to his hotel. It was nine in the morning.

"What else did you have in mind, son?"

"We have a status meeting in an hour and half. Doubt there will be anything new, but the next one isn't scheduled for two weeks, case gone cold and all that."

"I think that meeting is a fine idea. Then I can go take a long nap."

After John showed customs officer Brian Lucas his passport and Texas Ranger-Retired card, the only two things that the officer was interested in were John Menger's walking stick and his light-gray Stetson, both sitting atop his luggage.

"Now that is one shepherd's crook," said Officer Lucas. "Must be almost six feet long."

Well," said John, "it's more of a kill-a-rattler stick. You see, five footers are pretty common, and every now and then you meet one that is six feet or more." John took the stick and pushed one end out in front of him and onto the ground. "Gotta hit 'em right in the head before they strike."

John handed it to the officer. "This one's made of mesquite, a native Texas hardwood. Hard as nails."

"I've heard about this. Folks over here have started using it for outdoor cooking—your bar-be-cue."

"Slow burning. Use that and my sauce and you'll have the best grilled meat ever."

Officer Lucas then picked up the hat and turned it over, feeling it and studying it as if it was a strange artifact. "That, sir, is one nice topper," he told John.

"Go ahead. Try it on, sir," John told him. The man smiled and put the hat on his head. He and John laughed out loud. "Now all I need to do is get you up on a horse to make you an honorary Texan."

"Could I take a picture?" the customs official asked. John looked at George questioning.

George said, "He means with his phone."

John looked back at the official. "Fine with me." The man handed his cellphone to George. George took the picture and handed the cellphone back.

"Now that is amazing," John said. "So, it takes pictures too."

The officer took the hat off. Without checking any luggage and without any more questions, he said "You can go on through, sir, and thank you. Her Majesty welcomes you to the United Kingdom. Enjoy your stay."

John smiled and put his hat on, making him look a foot taller than he already was.

- § -

At the station, no one could remember if a man had ever walked in wearing a Stetson hat. John Menger was impressive, hat or no hat. George smiled at the people now staring, frozen in place, and at the silence that followed them into the main room.

More than a dozen people were there for the regular status meeting. Sixteen photos were mounted on a large board. They were before-and-after shots—alive and dead—of the eight victims. Separate lines connected each photo to the word cancer, to the word terminal, and to the words brain damage. No other lines went to all the photos.

John stared at the board for some moments. Everyone else was silent as they watched him. DCI Shope came in, and George introduced him to John.

"Captain John Menger, this is Detective Chief Inspector Shope," said George.

Shope extended his hand. "It's Alistair Shope, sir." DCI Shope did not say his entire name—Alistair Sean Shope. Neither did he mention the acronym that described his title, which was always used at the station. Shope had spoken earlier to Superintendent Argyle who had only glowing, almost mythical, things to say about John Menger.

"My pleasure," said John.

Shope looked at John and at those assembled. "This is Captain John Menger of the Texas Rangers, retired. Don't let the easy Texas drawl and the calm manner fool you. This is one good lawman as they say there, and one fine detective. He has come here to help us."

After the reports, which really weren't reports since there had been no new developments other than the identity of the eighth victim, Shope turned to John and asked him, "Sir, I understand you have had such a case before, and we would appreciate any suggestions you may have."

John looked at the board and then back at the people assembled in the room. "I appreciate your asking me, DCI, but I don't want to mosey in here and tell y'all how to work your cattle or mend your fences."

Shope smiled. "Sir, I heard a saying on one of your TV shows: 'This ain't his first rodeo.' I know you've ridden a few horses in your time, and you may have had some experiences that could help us. We are at eight dead ends."

"If I can, I would like to make one suggestion." John looked around the room. "By my count when I walked in, outside this room you have eleven personnel, and in here you've got fourteen. Could you ask each of them—all of them, I don't care what they do or what their rank is—could you ask each of them to think and do this: write down their thoughts if they have any, and let us have them back here for another meeting in forty-eight hours?"

"Yes?" Shope replied with a question in his voice.

"You see, y'all are at a standstill. There are twenty-five of y'all—ten women, fifteen men. By my rough reckoning, about half of y'all are thirty-five years of age or under. And each of you has been thinking about this case. Each of you knows some of the facts. Some of you have had thoughts and opinions no one else knows—maybe some intuitions, even guesses. I would just like everyone to imagine whatever they can and let's see where we go. Write down any ideas. And no one has to sign his or her name."

John was met with blank stares. "Look, you have no idea how often in history it is the new guy or the new gal who comes up with an idea—a solution or a way to do something. Just up the road here, you had those Watson and Crick guys, new to the scene, and they did what none of the old heads could do. They are the ones who came up with the actual structure of the DNA double helix, using a young Rosalind Franklin's amazing X-ray crystallography. Not the Cambridge dons, not the chubby tenured full professors. Watson and Crick, not any Oxford deans, got the Nobel Prize."

As John spoke, those assembled for the meeting looked at each other as if to say, "Is this your ordinary Texas cowboy?"

Shope knew that it was at least something that had not yet been done, although he had no hope. "Fine, then, think about it, write it down, be back here in two days."

John Menger turned to Shope. "Sir, is there a place or a room I could use to go over the documents and the evidence?"

"There are about twenty-eight boxes of documents and reports now, and some video and CCTV."

"CCTV?" asked John.

"We've got four hospitals, and they all have CCTV inside and out. Closed circuit television—video surveillance. About two million of them, public and private, all over the UK. So there are hours and hours of video. We've gone through it all and found nothing."

"Is it possible to see just the CCTV for two hours before each body was found, and for an hour after?"

George interrupted. "Sir, I can get him a laptop and some discs."

"And," asked John Menger, "can you teach me how to use this laptop?"

"Laptop. Yes, sir," said Shope.

"I appreciate that, DCI; but you don't need to call me sir. John is just fine. Like when I was in the US Army, we used to tell the new recruits, 'Don't call me sir. I work for a living.'" This brought more smiles than laughter from all those present who dared not fail to call DCI Shope sir.

Shope asked John, "Are you sure you don't want to go get some rest before you begin all this?"

"Sir, I don't sleep like I used to, and if I go to my hotel I will lie there and think about this case. Let me do some work here and get good and tired."

"George," said Shope, "get him one of the interrogation rooms no one is using. And start the documents coming."

- § -

"What's he doing in there?" asked one of the constables.

"He takes a pile of documents, looks at them one page at a time, and goes through about a box an hour or two. Some faster, some slower. But I don't have a clue what he's doing," said another constable.

John Menger was like a human scanner. He'd go through a box

and a half or so, then take a break, then go through another box and a half. Then he'd look at some video before going back to the boxes.

- § -

"Thank y'all," John Menger said, holding a stack of notes and papers. He had also reviewed several written suggestions from those working at the station. "I think this is going in the right direction. I suspect there are more than the eight victims you all have found so far." People in the room looked at each other and then back at John. "There are two suggestions here, one unsigned, one signed 'DSO'. The first unsigned one says that we are either missing something about someone we have interviewed or someone we have studied, or there is someone we have not yet realized is involved. I think this is true. I have read the reports on all the employees, all the doctors, all the nurses and technicians and staff. Right now, I don't think it is any of them. I could be wrong. And then this second note, signed by DSO—"

John was interrupted as two constables in uniform simultaneously said, "Detective Sergeant Mom!" When the laughter subsided, John asked, "And who is Mom?" Again there was laughter.

A small hand barely appeared over the head of one of the other detective sergeants. "That would be me, sir. Detective Sergeant O'Mara, Margaret Opal O'Mara." A short—very short—young lady moved around from behind the detective sergeant in front of her.

"Little lady," said John Menger, "good thing you didn't try to get in this outfit when Sir Bobby Peel had that five-foot-ten-inches-high rule for coppers." Laughter again ensued.

"Where we come from, you'd have to stand up to look a rattler in the eye. But good things come in small packages. May I read what you wrote down?"

"Yes, sir," said DS O'Mara smiling.

"We already know," John Menger read, "the suspect—or we don't. We already have information about him or her—or we don't. If we don't, this person has gone unnoticed and it may be that this person, unnoticed or not, has gone unchallenged. Someone who comes and goes who is not a hospital employee, and yet whose entry and exit are never questioned."

"Ma'am," said John Menger, "I think y'all have a saying over here—'spot on'—and after all I have seen, I think you are spot on."

Applause broke out with cries of "Yeah, Mom!" and D.S. O'Mara blushed.

John Menger began again, "Darlin' ..." He noticed the audible intake of breath of many in the room and knew immediately he had said something at least very interesting. He paused. Then he continued. "Folks, I'm too old to care about what you think about that, and at my age, and because I'm from Texas, I've got some kind of immunity."

DS O'Mara was smiling. "Go on, sir," she said.

John too smiled. "Like I was saying ... Darlin' ... after I read your note, then I went to your CCTV stuff and started watching the front doors. I mean the places where folks come into these hospitals, the sign-in stations and the lines and the security checks. And on February first this year, murder day for Susan Leister, starting at three in the afternoon, at your Sanderson Research Hospital in Warlingham, from then on you had forty-one people sign in at the desk. That's forty-one people who are not employees or anyone else who does not have to sign in. But I looked at the video, and here it is."

John motioned to Sergeant George to play the video on a laptop at the front of the room. "But forty-two people walked past that sign-in station." George played the video and then stopped it at the 5:20 p.m. point. There was a man bent over signing a daily sign-in log. "There!" said John.

One of the constables said, "So that's the man."

"Nope," said John. "Look here." He pointed to the edge of the video images. There was the hem of a white coat, a blue label showing, some clearly female legs, and some light-colored high-heel shoes."

"This is number forty-two. And those are not the shoes worn by a lady with a mop or a nurse who walks several miles an evening up and down the halls. And this is the time for shift change at Sanderson Research."

"A woman serial killer?" asked George. "I didn't know there was such a thing."

John Menger continued. "And as Detective Sergeant O'Mara said ..." John looked over at 'Mom,' acknowledging her contribution, " ... she does not sign in. She goes by the sign-in station, but she does not sign in. She does not go across the way where the employees walk in with their identity cards. She goes right past the sign-in station. Not unnoticed, but unchallenged just as Margaret said."

Detective Sergeant O'Mara was beaming, and some of her colleagues were giving her high fives and thumbs up.

"The shoes," said John. "Look at the shoes." Everyone stared and squinted at the laptop screen, and then George focused in and enlarged the shoes. They were a light color, maybe beige, and they were stylish.

"Those are Gianvito Ranatonis," said O'Mara.

"No plonk shoes for this lady," said one of the policemen in uniform."

"Chavs do not wear Rigatonis," said another.

"Right," said John. "Eight hundred bucks and up. What's that in pounds, George?"

"Just over six hundred and twenty or so, Captain Menger," said George.

"So, thank you, Mom, Darlin'!" John Menger grinned when he said it. "We've got someone to check out. Someone unchallenged. And for now, not a clue who she is."

DCI Shope was nodding his head up and down. "Well I am gobsmacked, John."

"Gobsmacked?" questioned John Menger.

"You know," interjected George, covering his open mouth with one hand. Still John Menger looked puzzled. George went on, "snookered, confused."

"Oh, you mean "flummoxed, bambozzled, disoriented," said John Menger, laughing.

"Well, ladies and gentlemen, let's get on with it. And let's review all the videos of all sign-ins for each murder."

"What else, John? Any suggestions?" asked DCI Shope.

"The shoes. Expensive. Who goes into a research hospital wearing such shoes? Not an average doctor. Not a nurse on nurse's pay. Not a technician. Not anyone who is going to be walking or standing for a whole shift. I would be surprised if even the doctors' wives have such shoes. And the brains—all of them, gelled. I read the reports. And all the bodies stiff as planks. There must be something else, something in common, for their brains to all end up like that. For them all to end up fully gelled so quickly."

"John," said DCI Shope, "Martin here can tell you all we've got." Shope looked at DS Martin Bairn.

"Sir," Bairn began, "the postmortems told us how they ended up, but nothing, not even a theory, on how they got that way. But death was almost instant, about as painless a way to go as being shot in the brain with a large-caliber bullet. Probably like dying in your sleep. So far, we know they all got painkillers. But their brains—like a whole container turning into Jell-O instantaneously. No explanation yet. They are doing more pharmacological tests."

"The devil?" said John. "Or a compassionate angel of death?"

"No way to tell, sir," said Bairn. "Perhaps they were quick because she wanted it to be quick. Perhaps the way it was done—about which we are indeed 'flummoxed'—isn't planned, but it does turn out that this gelling happened very quickly, in a few moments. Bam! Liquid to gel, like a freeze ray from a sci-fi movie."

John Menger was quiet, staring off into space. No one in the room spoke.

Bairn asked him, "The devil, sir?"

"Pharmakia," John said. "Root of pharmacy and pharmaceuticals. Greek word for sorcery, witchcraft, of the devil."

John shut his eyes for about twenty seconds. "Yes, quick," he said. "They all died quickly." He continued like a news report: "Susan Leister, dead at Sanderson Research Hospital, forty-four years old. You did have the witness, the one who confronted the person leaving Susan Leister's room. That day, those shoes were on her floor, on floor five. And they were there on floor five about an hour after the shoes went by the sign-in station."

John Menger continued. "That's when your first witness saw the person leaving Susan Leister's room. Dark hair, black clothes, white running shoes. That's why y'all started an investigation; that's why you called this one a murder. The shoes went past the sign-in station and weren't seen again. Shoes rushed out of Leister's room." John was reviewing video footage in his mind. "The person your witness saw leaving was a person, as your witness said, in white sneakers, black pants, and a black balaclava, black shirt, head down, black cap."

Leddemer found the right disc and inserted it in his computer. Video came up on a large screen. No one in the room had ever seen anything like this. There was the person leaving Leister's room.

"So it was quick. Your witness rushed in the room, and Leister was already dead, already planked." John focused on the people in the room. "Now we have some things to go on. Now, how do y'all say it? We can 'get cracking'?"

No one said a word. They simply stared at each other and then at Ranger Captain John Menger. DCI Shope started listing tasks to be done, lists to be checked, files to be retrieved, and persons to be interviewed.

John asked DCI Shope, "Can you get me all the hospital files on all the victims? And all the files on anyone else who has died there in the last two years on whom no post-mortem was done?"

"Will do, John, but you may be deluged."

"I can handle it," said John Menger, and no one laughed.

- § -

After another good night's sleep, which erased what was left of his jet lag, John Menger was back at the Caterham station in the interrogation room, going through documents and watching CCTV video. At around seven in the evening, D.S. O'Mara looked in and asked, "Feel like a break and some dinner?"

John was pleased for the interruption. "Sounds good, little lady. What did you have in mind?"

"There's a pub—that's a 'public house'—a few streets from here that has the usual drinks, but also has very good food. Quite unusual for an English pub. It's called The Dog Star."

"You're on." John stood up, picked up his walking stick, and walked out of the room. Sergeant George Leddemer was at his desk, looking at his computer screen. John asked DS O'Mara, "Want to see if George is hungry?"

"Sure," said Margaret. "George …"

George looked over at John and Margaret. "Fancy some food with us?" Margaret asked.

"Yes, I'm starving. And I'm tired of looking at hospital files online. My eyeballs are useless."

- § -

They got a table in the middle of the pub. John sat with his back to the bar, facing a wall covered in a full-length mirror. Margaret was to his right, and George, to his left. John placed his walking stick so it leaned against the table.

"Sir," said Margaret, "do you mind if I ask you about your memory?"

"No, ma'am, and you don't need to call me sir. John is just fine."

Margaret and George looked at each other, both knowing that they could not drop the sir very easily.

"The memory." John paused. "Well, it's like you remember how to type, or use your computer keyboard commands. It's almost as if your arms and fingers know all by themselves what to do and how to do it. I can't explain my memory, but it's like it's there and I do it. They told me it is usually children who have it, and then they lose it. Mine kind of hung around. Doesn't bother me. I can pay attention to it or not."

"And you still recall everything?"

"Well, don't know about that, especially now I just turned seventy. But here's an example. Eighth grade—that's about like thirteen-year-olds over here—Sister Mary Fidelis had us all write a poem. Poems weren't really my thing, so I started reading a book. She saw me and asked me to recite my poem. Made one up on the spot about Sirius, brightest star in the sky, and said it right there. Today I still remember that poem, every word. Thought of it when we came in here. That star is in the Canis Major constellation."

George and Margaret looked at each other.

"And that star, Sirius, is also called the Dog Star."

The doors to The Dog Star opened and some young men came into the pub.

"Who are they?" John asked.

"Local punks," said George. Leader's name's Pinkie Black, and the other two thugs do his bidding."

Pinkie and his men sauntered in and went up to the bar along the side of the room behind John. After Pinkie was served a pint, he left his stool and came over and stood between John and Margaret.

"Hello, sweetheart." He addressed Margaret with his back to John. Margaret did not even look up at him.

"How about you come over and have a drink with me and my boys?"

Looking up, Margaret said, "No thank, you." Then she looked away.

"I'm really not the sort who takes no for an answer," he told Margaret.

John looked at Pinkie and said, "Young man, the little lady has said no, and I think's it's no."

Without turning his body, Pinkie glanced back at John. "Shut up, you old git. They should have taught you some manners where you're from."

John made no visible reaction to Pinkie's words.

Pinkie turned back to Margaret. Putting his hand on her shoulder, he said, "Just one drink, and you'll like us."

"Please remove your hand," Margaret said.

John Menger was not smiling. "Son, where I'm from is Texas, and we did learn some manners there. In Texas when a lady has told you no, it is no. Please walk away before I walk you away."

Pinkie laughed out loud and reached out again, putting one hand under Margaret's arm as if to help her up. "Get lost, old man! This is none of your business." Pinkie moved to backhand John across the face.

Most folks with any knowledge of the history of pugilism agree that the greatest boxer of all time—The Greatest—was Cassius Clay, who was later known as Muhammad Ali. And most of them agree that his physical condition, and his "reach" coupled with his lighting speed—25 percent faster than Sugar Ray Robinson's clocked speed, one of the fastest until Clay came on the scene—were his most potent weapons. In his prime, he could hit an opponent five times in one second. And they also agree that another one of his many very lethal weapons was his size: six feet three inches tall and around 236 pounds. John Menger had an inch on Clay in height and an inch on him in reach. And he had not yet lost all his response speed.

John avoided Pinkie's hand. It was an easy move to bring the walking stick up and leverage the top end against Pinkie's face, even from a sitting position.

Pinkie Black was unconscious before his head hit the floor. The powerful blow from the walking stick had caught him full between his nose and his jaw, and his jaw was broken. His slumping body landed up against the bar between his two fellow punks. They stared at Pinkie and then both looked at John Menger. John saw them in the mirror and was up before they got to him. George and Margaret were also up, but the two punks had eyes only for John.

It was as if John's arms, hands, and body instantly remembered what they had learned all those years ago at Fort Benning, Georgia, in US Army Ranger training and at Ft. Bragg, North Carolina, with the Green Berets. The thug to the right had a chain out and ready, and the one to the left had drawn a knife. John caught the chain with his right hand and simultaneously parried the knife with his left arm. He pulled on the chain, ramming that thug's jaw into his right fist, crushing bone. He let go of the chain and swung around. His right fist recoiled from the jaw of the punk with the chain and rammed into the other's chin. In a moment, both attackers were on the ground in pain. Pinkie was still unconscious on the floor, up against the bar.

John looked at them and then at Margaret and George who were staring wide-eyed at this calm old man. He smiled. "Can we get some food now?" he asked.

- § -

The next morning when John walked into the Caterham station main room, George pushed the play button on a video on his laptop, and Jimmy Dean sang " … and a crashin' blow from a huge right hand sent a Lousiana fella to the promised land, Big John." Everyone there applauded.

DCI Shope approached John. "Do you know how much paperwork you have made me do?" he asked with a smile. "And the three broken jaws do not make it one whit easier. Good thing it's all on video, or I'd have to send you for sensitivity training and community relations education. Or I'd have to worry about laying criminal charges against you."

- § -

In a sitting room in Buckingham Palace, Prince Philip looked up from a newspaper and addressed Elizabeth. "John Menger is in the UK, in Surrey, my dear. He appears to be up to his old self and enjoying his time with us."

The queen looked up from a book and smiled. With a wistful, faraway look, all she said was, "John."

"Don't you think we should see him while he is here?" Philip asked.

"By all means. Remind me tomorrow morning."

- § -

The status meeting began with George Leddemer reporting on what they had learned in several interviews of hospital employees and staff members. It was true that the employees at the sign-in desk at Sanderson Research Hospital routinely waved several folks through without checking ID badges and without requiring them to sign in.

"We took into consideration the shoes and eliminated everyone except four people." George reached for the first of four photos and put it up on a board. "Dr. Mary Coel. Thirty-two years old. CEO LongLamp Technologies. Does medical instrument start-ups. Has done three successfully in the past dozen years. LongLamp has done three levels of investment. She is rich and will likely become richer. Goes to Sanderson Research and all the other hospitals where victims have died regularly. Deals with doctors, nurses, and researchers using LongLamp's experimental fiber-optic real-time cell analysers."

George put the second photo up. "Dr. Anne Mynatt. Doctor. Oncologist. Has patients at three of our death hospitals. Her salary is a typical doctor's pay, but her husband is Sir Henry Frederic Howard Fitzwilliam of London, the Fourth, MP, member of parliament. She did Oxford, Cambridge, and all that.

"Number three," George continued, placing a third photo on the board, "is Ms. Jane Gerveen. Not doctor. A representative for VitalCare Pharma. She goes to all the hospitals. Sees doctors, nurses, and researchers. Peddles VitalCare's regular drugs and promotes experimental ones. Makes about two hundred thousand quid a year. Can certainly afford the shoes."

"Fourth and not least," said Geroge, "is Dr. Elizabeth Royceston. Head administrator Sanderson Research. Independently wealthy. Widowed young. At the top of her profession. Known as a crusader for cancer patients' rights. No-nonsense, do-the-job-and-do-it-now type."

"So what do they have in common?" asked DCI Shope.

One of the male detective sergeants said, "Bit of all right."

Another chimed in, "Bad kitties all."

A third said, "Bagsy on the blondes." And all the men in the room agreed.

"Yes," said John Menger. "All lookers. All four, handsome women. That's the main reason they walk on by. Am I right, DS O'Mara?" By the question, John was paying a compliment to DS O'Mara's insight that this person came and went unchallenged.

DS O'Mara was pleased. "Yes, sir. Yes. Once the men got to know her, they would wave her on through every time."

Turning to Shope, John said, "How do we do this? Check them

out? Go to where they work and talk to them? Bring them here for questioning? Caution them? Arrest them? What do y'all do these days?"

Shope thought for a second. "Let's do some more research and then see where we go."

John Menger nodded his head. He already had a primary suspect, but he said nothing. He needed more facts, more evidence.

George Leddemer looked over at John Menger. "You know, they have something else in common. They all have the names of queens of England."

You could see the wheels turning and the memory coming on. John thought for a few seconds and then said. "I see. Yes, if you accept the nine-day reign of Lady Jane Grey in 1553. Very good, George."

- § -

John had watched the interviews with the four women who had ties to all the hospitals and research facilities where patients had been killed. Throughout each of the interviews, he had listened and suggested questions as he observed through the mirrored glass. None of the interviews was short. Each had lasted over two hours and had included the usual general questions and then specific questions related to the times of each of the murders. Two of the doctors had actually treated several of the victims. The total interview time for all of them was over nine and a half hours.

All four women apparently had alibis for all eight murders.

"The only one," John said to DS O'Mara and DCI Shope after the last interview was concluded, "whose alibi we cannot check against facility records, with companions, or from phone records is Ms. Gerveen, who says she attended that conference last year."

O'Mara looked at Shope as if to say, How does he know that? How does he do that?

John realized he needed to explain. "These folks all said they were in such and such a place on duty or with someone else doing something when each of the murders occurred. We can check all these alibis. Might as well get their phone records too. Time records, sign-in registers, camera tapes—I'm assuming these will corroborate the work time, and your people can meet with each person the women referred to for alibis for those time periods when they said they were with someone. You probably have them coming and going on camera with times and date stamps. But that conference last year? Ms. Gerveen claims to have attended that alone. I've seen no video of that conference."

"Did she say that?" asked Shope.

John thought for a few moments. "Yes, during her interview last Thursday, in the afternoon, she said she attended the opening of the conference on May eighteenth—alone."

Shope and O'Mara stared at John.

"It was a Friday. Day before the May nineteenth murder at Sanderson."

- § -

A week later, DCI Shope placed a pile of papers and files in front of John in the interrogation room that had become John's home away from home.

"All there. Everyone's stories checked out. All the alibis good. And now we have"—Shope pointed to the laptop John was using—"the video footage from that May eighteenth conference last year. If that checks out, we are back to zip. Zilch."

John stared at the computer screen. "All three days there?"

The conference went from Friday afternoon to Sunday brunch.

"Not only all there, but multiple cameras from all over the hotel interior and exterior. Somewhat more boring than watching *Star Wars*."

John knew the answer would be interesting. "Star wars?"

"You really are a hermit, aren't you, John?" Shope asked. "*Star Wars*. By many accounts, the most paradigm-rending science fiction movie of all time. You'd really like Yoda."

"Not even going to ask," said John.

By the time Shope left, John had already begun to review the tapes from the conference hotel.

- § -

Shope and O'Mara were beyond expectant. "So, you've found something?"

"Here you are. May eighteenth, five in the afternoon. Ms. Jane Gerveen signs in." John turned the laptop around for them. "And here"—he clicked a button—"here, she retrieves her name tag."

Margaret was disheartened. "So she was there."

John smiled. "Now watch as she walks away from the sign-in area to the elevators."

Jane Gerveen was easy to pick out in the cluster of people milling and moving around in the video, but Shope and Margaret noticed nothing.

"Let me play that again for y'all," said John.

Margaret focused now on the screen and watched Jane Gerveen walk away.

"Shoes! It's the shoes!" she yelled out loud as she recognized the Gianvito Ranatonis Jane Gerveen was wearing.

"Right you are, darlin'." John continued, "And that's not all. From Saturday morning around eight 'til Saturday evening around eleven, she is not in any footage. Not at any meeting or seminar. Not at any meal. Not at any bar."

"So she could have driven back, killed the patient, and then returned," exclaimed Margaret.

"No, she did not do that. You can check the parking area for yourselves. Her car was there all the time. She didn't get back in it 'til Sunday."

Margaret was deflated.

"But here!" John put a new video up on the screen. "Here is the local train station. Nine on Saturday morning. Ms. Gerveen buys a ticket home. Looks like round trip, but you can check that for sure later. It is her."

"So, she takes a train back, does the murder, and returns," said Shope.

"Spot on," said John. "And here she is at three in the afternoon getting off the return train."

The screen showed Ms. Jane Gerveen, clear as day, walking from a train and going out through the station.

"You should check with all the cabbies. No way she walked all the way to the hotel."

"All we have is confirmation that she left the hotel and returned. We don't know where she went. We don't know why. And we can't take the big leap that she is our murderer. We have no motive. None."

"If we bring her in again, it looks like it must be 'under caution,' and there go all the red flags." Turning to John she said, "You didn't get us this far to hit a brick wall, sir. What do you think?"

John was silent for a few moments. "Easy on that 'sir,' little lady. We are fellow officers. I'm John."

DS O'Mara looked down and then looked up. "Yes, sir—John," she said with a laugh.

"Do you have enough to search her house and office with what we know so far? I think we get her back in—under caution or however you do it. She is very intelligent. If she's our man, she's got this far on smarts. So we let her talk. Ask her the real open-ended questions. She'll think she can talk us away from the real trail. And we let her wait several times. Maybe I'm in there. Now there's a surprise."

Shope agreed. "Time to engage. O'Mara?"

"I agree."

"Then you're the lead," said Shope. "Woman to woman."

"Do we have enough for a search warrant?" asked John.

"This one's on the edge. We go for it and see what happens."

- § -

"She came voluntarily," Shope told John as Ms. Jane Gerveen was being escorted to an interrogation room at the Caterham Station. "She left her house as they were serving the search warrant and came peaceably."

Before Ms. Gerveen got to the door to the interrogation room, a man entered the corridor and walked quickly to catch up to her. He introduced himself to Shope and to John. "Frederick Eynsford-Hill," he said, extending his hand to John. "Ms. Gerveen's counsel."

"John Menger," said John.

Turning to Shope, he said, "Good to see you again, Alistair. It is always a pleasure to work with you."

FEH, as Mr. Eynsford Hill was known around the courts and the Caterham Station, had often defended the accused when the detective work had been done by Shope and the other officers there.

Once they were all seated in the room, Mr. Eynsford-Hill asked Shope, "And who is Mr. Menger? What is his capacity here?"

"He's Her Majesty's consultant in these matters. Also a retired Texas Ranger," replied Shope.

FEH appeared taken aback. "Fine" was all he said.

Shope began the recording of the interrogation, noting all present in the room and informing Ms. Gerveen of her rights not to reply to the questions and that she was 'under caution.' DS O'Mara was in the observation room.

Shope started with the usual informational questions. Then the door to the room opened, and a uniformed officer brought in some evidence bags. When they were set on the table, Ms. Gerveen turned to whisper to her counsel, and they engaged in a short conversation.

Shope then handed over item QE 234, which was a small tote bag with the initials 'JAG' embroidered on it. "Ms. Gerveen, what is your middle name?"

FEH whispered to Ms. Gerveen.

"No comment," she replied.

Shope paused. "It is Agatha, isn't it?"

"No comment."

Then he handed her the other item. "I am now handing Ms. Gerveen item QE 47. The transparent bag contained a woman's dark-brunette wig.

"No comment," said Ms. Gerveen.

Shope picked up another one of the bags. "Each item I have shown you so far is from the search of your house. Here is another. I now show you what has been marked as item QE 28 and ask you if you can tell me what these are." The bag contained white athletic shoes.

"No comment," said Ms. Gerveen.

Shope picked up another one of the bags. "I now show you what has been marked as item QE 5 and ask you if you can tell me what these are." The bag contained beige Gianvito Ranatoni shoes.

"No comment," said Ms. Gerveen.

Shope looked at John and then back to Ms. Gerveen. "Let's take a break. It's eleven fifteen a.m." Shope turned off the recording equipment.

FEH looked at Ms. Gerveen and then turned to Shope. "It is going to be 'no comment' from here on, Alistair. If you have questions you have to ask and get no reply from Ms. Gerveen, I suggest we get on with that after this break so she can put her 'no comment' on record and we can be done."

"Freddy," said Shope, "always Mr. Efficient and Mr. No Comment. Thanks for the heads up."

After Shope asked what he thought was the last question, again the door to the room opened and DS Bairn entered. He handed Shope two documents.

"Tox report," he whispered to Shope. "Painkiller, yes, and they felt no pain. But also TripSeis, a VitalCare Pharma experimental drug that was never approved. Administered after the painkillers."

"What else?" asked Shope, fingering the second document.

Quietly, Bairn told Shope, "Almost three years ago, both her parents, mum and dad, had weeks, maybe months, to live. Both died taking part in a VitalCare experimental program to prove the efficacy and safety of TripSeis. She was with each of them as they died. Bodies ended up just like all the eight we have been investigating. They got painkillers—not like our victims, though. They got theirs too late. They went through the agony caused by the drug."

Shope turned to Ms. Gerveen, who had been looking intently at the two documents that had been given to Shope.

"Ms. Gerveen, do you know what caused your parents' deaths?"

FEH turned and stared at Ms. Gerveen. She bowed her head.

After some moments, she looked up and said, "No comment," as she fought back tears.

"No more questions," Shope announced. "Now, Ms. Gerveen, I am placing you under arrest for the murders of these eight persons." Shope read the list of the victims' names. Ms. Gerveen listened without showing any emotion.

John looked at the mirror wall without smiling, letting DS O'Mara know he believed she had played a major role in the arrest.

"I would like to speak alone with my client before I leave," said FEH.

"Take whatever time you need, Freddy. Let her know that this is crystal. You will get all the evidence we have. Consider very seriously the plea she will make."

"Alistair, all courtesies much appreciated," said FEH.

The two constables who had entered the room, along with John and Shope, exited and left Ms. Gerveen with her counsel. Later she was escorted to processing and then placed in a holding cell.

- § -

Some months later, after Ms. Gerveen's not guilty plea, the trial began with widespread press coverage in every media. There was worldwide interest in the trial, and all the streets around the courthouse had to be closed due to the TV vans and reporters everywhere.

Very early on in the proceedings, a woman exiting the courtroom told the reporters, "It's not just eight! It's many more."

Headlines made it known that there had been more victims than the police first suspected—eleven more, with more investigations still ongoing. The total was nineteen. All had been cancer patients, and all were living with a prognosis of death within weeks or months. All were given painkillers and rendered unconscious. Then they all died from a massive dose of TripSeis administered intravenously.

The only response to all the inquiries made to VitalCare Pharma was a consistent "No comment."

- § -

"I don't like it," said Mrs. Justice Martina Brett. "Not at all." For the fourth time in four days, the jury had informed the judge that they were unable to reach a verdict. The following week, the judge declared a mistrial.

"I would encourage the prosecution to make a decision on seeking a retrial as soon as possible and to communicate the decision promptly to this court," said the judge.

Frederick Eynsford-Hill turned to Jane Gerveen without saying a word, without even a hint of a smile.

- § -

John, Shope, and DS O'Mara were walking down a hallway, away from the courtroom, when John heard a voice behind him. "Ranger Menger! John Menger," the female voice said. It was Jane Gerveen. She approached John as her attorney whispered to her that it was not a good idea to speak with him.

John turned around. "Yes, ma'am?"

"Can we talk for a moment?"

John said, "Yes, ma'am. As far as I know that it not against your law."

"I just wanted to thank you."

John had heard a great many defendants talk and say a great many things over his career, but this surprised him. He did not reply.

Jane Gerveen continued. "I have heard about your fine work. All the publicity about this is down to you. So thank you."

John's mind raced, and then he realized what had happened and what was happening. "You're are most welcome," he said. "Back home we say, de nada—it is nothing."

"No, sir, it is not nothing," said Jane Gerveen. "And I appreciate all you have done." With that, she turned and walked away with her attorney.

DS O'Mara stared at her and then asked John, "What did she mean by that?"

"Little lady, I think you just heard a sincere thank you. I think this is exactly how she wanted this to play out. I think she was, in her mind, easing the pain of all these terminally ill—really terminal—patients. She was also exposing the disastrous effects of that drug and what had been kept secret about the real results of the experimental testing and the drug trials. And a new trial would suit her down to the ground. There would be more publicity."

"I'm amazed," said DCI Shope.

- § -

Within a week of the mistrial, VitalCare Pharma stock collapsed, losing over 95 percent of its value. Its four top officers were stopped at London Luton Airport boarding the company's private jet, for which no flight plan had been registered. The company's assistant CFO was found at her apartment, an apparent suicide.

- § -

John was back in his hotel room and had everything packed for the plane ride home. The phone in the room rang.

"Sir, there is a man here at the front desk. He is from The Palace—Buckingham Palace!—and he would like to speak with you."

John made his way down to the lobby.

"Mr. John Menger?" the man asked with the utmost courtesy and a with evident respect.

"Yes, sir."

"Sir Philip Lucas." He extended his hand. After they shook hands, he told John, "I have a request for you from Her Majesty." He handed John an envelope.

"Can we go now?" John said, after reading the note contained in the envelope.

"So glad you agree, sir. I am under royal command not to take no for an answer. Yes, please come with me. We have a car waiting."

- § -

From the time they left the Rolls Royce sedan, which had stopped in the porte cochere on a side of the palace, until they stood outside a large room in the palace's interior, everyone bowed as John passed, and many smiled. He strode on with Sir Lucas, unawed by what would have rendered most people stunned and silent.

Sir Lucas walked past the men on either side of the door and announced, "Your highness, Captain John Menger, from Texas."

The queen had been sitting down, but she immediately rose, violating the palace protocol, not waiting for John Menger, from Texas, to come to her.

John approached her, smiling, and then he bowed. "My Lady," was all he said as Prince Philip stood behind the queen.

"So, the rules say you may not touch me." She laughed. "And if you were my subject, I would order you to hug me. Since you are one of the rebels, I will request it." The queen laughed out loud as she and John embraced. Several of the men and women in the room looked at each other in utter disbelief.

John stood back, and Philip extended his hand. "So good to see you again, John. You know you have upset my bride by coming to her kingdom and not letting us know."

"I figured y'all had a lot to keep you busy ruling a kingdom and all that. Like we say back home, busier than a one-legged man in a butt-kicking contest. So I decided not to call."

"And if you do it again, sir," interrupted Elizabeth, "then we shall be very displeased." She turned and motioned to one of her assistants and whispered to her. Then she asked John, "Can we get you any refreshment?"

"No, Ma'am. I am just fine and really happy to see you again. It has been some years." Looking around the large room, he continued. "And I am glad you're back to a place with some nicer accommodations."

"Yes," said Philip. "This is not exactly like that island paradise where you saved her life."

"That was a two-way street, sir," John said. "And you know I owe her my life."

John thought back to that island all those years ago. The plane crash. The jihadi terrorists. And his comrade in arms, Her Majesty, Elizabeth II, queen of the United Kingdom. *Now that's one tall Texas tale*, he thought.

The queen's assistant had returned to the room carrying a framed picture.

"Remember you let me copy that photograph your father gave you?" asked the queen. "The one from 1944?" She handed John the enlarged black-and-white, somewhat faded photograph.

John took the frame and thought the young girl next to his father sure was pretty. "Yes, Ma'am, a good memory of a good man, and a lovely young girl."

- § -

On his way in a taxi to Heathrow Airport, John took out his wallet and removed a wrinkled picture. He thought back to that island, those days with "Liz," the horde of jihadi terrorists, and her saving his life. Yes, he thought, one tall tale. It was a photo of a bombardier/navigator of the B-17 Flying Fortress named Home James, 401st Bomb Group–Heavy, 8th Air Force, stationed in Deenthorpe, England. Along the bottom was the handwritten date June 9, 1944. A teenage girl stood next to his dad outside a dance club in London, and both were smiling.

When John got to the airport, George Leddemer and Margaret O'Mara met him at the check-in desk.

"Here to see me off?" John asked them.

George looked at Margaret. She remained silent.

"Sir," said George, "I know—we all know—you want to get home to that hellish heat and people who speak so you can understand them, but DCI Shope has asked me to ask you if you could ... how do you say it? ... 'see your way clear' to help us one more time before you go back."

Margaret began to speak when she saw that John was reluctant to say yes. "We've got three dead bodies and four dead dogs, and no clue how to solve this one."

John looked down at his carryon bag and thought of his dog back home. He smiled, and for a few moments, he simply stared silently at George and "Mom."

"George, do you still have that fancy phone?"

"Yes, sir."

"Get your DCI on it and tell him John Menger says there are two conditions: One, my friend Jose Onofrio Santo Estavara comes here. Two, he walks my dog straight through UK customs, no quarantine. I will then consider staying and helping y'all. But just this one last time."

Jesus Bring Me Home

It's not Gospel unless you sing it.
It's not love until you bring it.
It's not faith 'til you believe in His word.

It's not good news unless you bear it.
It's not hope until you share it.
It's salvation when you say, "Yes, Jesus, Lord."

Move me, Jesus. Bring me on home.
I've left the path and been alone.
Put me on that road going back home to you.
Move me, Jesus. Bring me on home.
I've left the path and walked alone.
Jesus, I need that road going back home to you.

I've left the straight and narrow,
Left your love that's oh so wide.
I've been a slave to sin, stood tall in my pride.
I've been dyin', I need your livin',
Need your love and your forgivin'.
Move me, Jesus. Bring me back by your side.

It's not Gospel unless you sing it.
It's not love until you bring it.
It's not faith 'til you believe in the Word.

It's not good news unless you bear it.
It's not hope until you share it.
It's salvation when you say, "Yes, Jesus, Lord."
It's salvation when you say, "Jesus is Lord."
It's salvation when you say, "Jesus, Jesus, Lord!"

CPSIA information can be obtained
at www.ICGtesting.com
Printed in the USA
BVHW030947030220
571273BV00009B/120